Ans	_____	M.L.	_____
ASH	_____	MLW	_____
Bev	_____	Mt.Pl	_____
C.C.	_____	NLM	_____
Dick	_____	Ott	_____
DRZ	_____	PC	_____
ECH	_____	PH	_____
ECS	_____	P.P.	_____
Gar	_____	Pion.P.	_____
GRM	_____	Q.A.	_____
GSP	_____	Riv	_____
G.V.	_____	Ross	_____
Har	_____	S.C.	_____
JPCP	_____	St.A.	_____
KEN	_____	St.J	_____
K.L.	_____	St.Joa	_____
K.M.	_____	St.M.	_____
L.H.	_____	Sgt	_____
LO	_____	T.H.	_____
Lyn	_____	TLLO	_____
L.V.	_____	T.M.	_____
McC	_____	T.T.	_____
McG	_____	Ven	_____
McQ	_____	VP	_____
MIL	_____	Wat	_____
	_____	Wed	_____
	_____	WIL	_____

HOLD ME FOREVER

To her fellow vacationers at the Meadow Spring dude ranch, Kate Weaver is just another tourist. Or is she? Ranch foreman Gil Singleton suspects otherwise. But even he has no way of guessing the truth about Kate, just as she has no way of knowing that she could fall hopelessly in love with Gil when the two of them find themselves fighting for survival in Colorado's untamed high country!

JANET WHITEHEAD

◆

HOLD ME FOREVER

Complete and Unabridged

LINFORD
Leicester

First published in Great Britain in 2008

First Linford Edition
published 2009

British Library CIP Data

Whitehead, Janet, *1958* –
Hold me forever
- -(Linford romance library)
1. Ranch managers- -Colorado- -Fiction.
2. Colorado- -Fiction. 3. Love stories.
4. Large type books.
I. Title II. Series
823.9'14–dc22

ISBN 978–1–84782–721–0

Published by
F. A. Thorpe (Publishing)
Anstey, Leicestershire

Set by Words & Graphics Ltd.
Anstey, Leicestershire
Printed and bound in Great Britain by
T. J. International Ltd., Padstow, Cornwall

This book is printed on acid-free paper

This is for David.
May he hold *me* forever!

1

Crouching in the cover of some rocks, Kate Weaver thought with disbelief, *Someone's trying to kill me! Someone is actually trying to kill me!*

She should have prepared herself for such an eventuality, of course. After all, the possibility had always been there. But somehow she'd never truly believed that it would come to this.

Even now she could hardly believe it. It *had* been a gunshot, hadn't it? Her horse had obviously thought so, because the animal had reared up in fright and thrown her to the talus with which the mountain slope was covered.

She had fallen hard and the horse had galloped away with its reins trailing, leaving her all alone, until some half-understood survival instinct had sent her scrabbling for the cover of a patch of weathered grey rocks.

After that there had been just silence, but for her quick, frightened breathing.

She listened for any other sounds, but heard nothing. Aside from an eagle soaring high overhead, she was alone — so far as she knew.

But what if she *wasn't?* What if her unseen assailant was even now creeping up on her, intent on finishing the job for good?

Kate knew a brief but all-consuming moment of pure, blind fear. For that giddying instant it threatened to overwhelm her, and she only managed to calm herself with effort.

She glanced around and winced. The fall had bruised her shoulders. But as near as she could tell, she really *was* alone now.

She wouldn't break cover just yet, though. Better to stay right where she was and do her best to recover first, just in case.

So she remained hidden, still wondering if the report she had heard was indeed a gunshot, and whether or not it really *had* been aimed at her. And while she waited, her thoughts turned back twenty-four hours, as she sought to discover just how she'd come to end up in such a predicament.

★ ★ ★

The moment she'd gotten her first look at Meadow Spring Ranch, Kate had thought, *I hope I can do this. I really don't want to let anyone down.*

About ninety minutes earlier, three bright red Chevrolet Tahoes had collected her and her fellow vacationers from the airport. There had been twelve all told, including a pair of newlyweds, a couple with two boisterous children, an older, retired couple and two young men in their late teens or early twenties, who had introduced themselves as Dan Collins and Joe Fulford.

Soon the city had fallen behind them and the long journey out to the dude ranch got underway. The trucks, weighed down with passengers and luggage, laboured across rolling prairies of wind-swept grama grass, the unyielding flatness of the land broken here and there by stands of cottonwood or lodgepole pine. Above them the wide Colorado sky was a near-perfect blue, the day itself warm, the air dry and clear.

Ahead, the road stretched arrow-straight between great plains bordered by yucca, cone flowers and sagebrush, and as she admired the scenery, the doubts which had plagued her on the short flight out began to recede. She had always wanted to see the west — the wild west of a million books and movies, that was — and this week at Meadow Spring certainly seemed to promise that.

But it also promised intrigue and, quite possibly, if things went horribly wrong for her, the very real chance of danger.

She was sitting in the passenger seat of the first pickup in the little convoy, beside a slope-shouldered man wearing a wide-brimmed Stetson. At the airport

4

he had introduced himself as Randall Woodward, and though she hated to admit it, she had taken an instant dislike to him, though she couldn't for the life of her really say why.

He was somewhere in his mid-thirties, which made him about ten years older than Kate, and he had a round, weathered face with a soft, clean-shaven jaw. He was of average height and stocky build, but in his checked shirt and riveted jeans, he looked every inch a cowboy.

'So,' he began, his voice a low drawl. 'What brings you to Meadow Spring? Not often we get such a pretty little lady coming way out here all by herself.'

'My mother died when I was very young,' Kate replied cryptically.

Woodward threw her a frown. 'I don't follow.'

'Well, my dad's a good man, but he only ever had two passions in life — his job, and the Old West. He's always been crazy about it. So instead of fairy tales, my bedtime stories were nearly always about cowboys and Indians. I guess that love of the west eventually rubbed off on me, too.'

'So you decided to come and see it all for yourself, is that it?'

'Something like that.'

He glanced at her again, saw a petite girl in a dark blue shirt with buttoned pockets and tailored khaki pants, with short, texture-cut auburn hair and a tip-tilted nose set well between large eyes the colour of mountain stream water.

'Didn't your boyfriend want to come along for the experience?' he asked, fishing none-too-subtly for more information.

Her voice turned cool when she replied, 'I don't *have* a boyfriend.'

'I find that hard to believe. A girl like you has *got* to have a man around someplace, surely?'

'No,' she told him, and still there was a hint of ice in her tone.

Hornless red and black cattle were

sprinkled across the fields, standing singly and in groups. They watched the three Tahoes go by without noticeable interest.

Then her attention was taken by a tiny dot high above the road ahead. Even as she watched, it wheeled and turned, a creature of infinite grace as it rode the thermals.

'Eagle,' supplied Woodward, following her gaze. 'You'll see plenty of them in these parts.' He showed big, yellow teeth briefly in a grin. 'Rattlesnakes, too. Them, and garter snakes.'

Warming to the subject, he continued, 'We got funnel-web spiders and jumpers, cellar spiders, wolf spiders, black widows, tarantulas, scorpions — '

Kate arched one eyebrow at him. 'You wouldn't by any chance be trying to *spook* me, would you, Mr Woodward?'

'It's Randy,' he replied. 'And no, ma'am. I wouldn't dare. But happen you get nervous or lonely any time over the next week, day or night . . . '

'I get the message,' she told him. 'But just so you know, I'm not looking for a holiday romance. All I want is some quiet time.'

'That's fair enough,' he allowed. 'But the offer still stands.'

They had entered an enormous basin of land by this time, and the countryside was almost more than she could take in. The colours of the flowers with which the fields were dotted were so deep they seemed almost fluorescent: shooting star columbine with its crimson wisps of flame, the resplendent yellow of tall cone flowers, the pale primrose of Blue Star, and off-white mouse-ear chickweed, standing tall on its green stems like flakes of half-fallen snow.

As breathtaking as this vista was, however, it was as nothing compared to the scene which presented itself to them as the Tahoe crested a broken ridge thirty minutes later. For there, below her, lay the magnificent valley in which Meadow Spring Ranch itself was nestled.

The ranch buildings occupied a sweeping saddle of land between two rolling hills covered in wheatgrass and crowned by extensive belts of aspen and juniper. It was a scattering of log structures and corrals of various sizes, built around a central yard. Away to the east, nine homely cabins lined the shore of a wide, sun-dappled lake.

However, Meadow Spring was dominated by the main house itself, a rambling construction with a low-pitched gable roof upon which had been built a series of additional A-framed rooms. Along the front of the house, a covered porch threw shade across a neat stone patio, where colourful trailing plants spilled their emerald fronds from large terracotta pots.

It was now, seeing not only the immensity of the ranch but of the country in which it was situated, that Kate began to understand for the first time the size of the job she'd taken on.

Ninety thousand acres ... it had

seemed a lot, even to a girl who wasn't completely sure just how big an *acre* was. But now, to actually *see* it first-hand . . .

I hope I can do this. I really don't want to let anyone down.

Then the three Tahoes wheeled into the yard and braked before the main house, where a pleasant, middle-aged couple dressed ranch-style were coming out into the bright afternoon sunshine to open car doors and greet the new intake of guests, and for a while after that there was no more time for misgivings.

The man, who was of average height and a little overweight, came hurrying around the leading Tahoe to help Kate out. He had thinning blond hair that was just turning to grey, and warm blue eyes that crinkled around the edges whenever he smiled, which seemed to be practically all the time. A shaggy moustache adorned his upper lip.

''Afternoon, Miss . . . ?'

'Weaver. Kate Weaver.'

He nodded and gave her right hand a brief, strong grasp. 'Well, we don't stand on ceremony here at Meadow Spring, so I'll call you Kate, lessen you got any objections, and you can call me Glenn. I'm Glenn Keyes, by the way. I own this place.'

'Please to meet you, Mr — '

'Uh, uh, uh.'

'Sorry. *Glenn*. It sure is a lovely place you've got here.'

'It is that. And I'm sure you'll have a good visit. My wife over there, Blanche, me and her'll make sure you do.' He turned at the waist and searched around until he spotted a cowhand who was sorting hackamores over by one of the two corrals. '*Gil!*'

The man he'd called looked up from what he'd been doing, then came over. The hard, physical life of the working cowboy had whittled him down to muscle and bone. Consequently, he was tall and lean, with wide shoulders that tapered gradually to a slim waist and a flat belly. He was dressed in a white bibbed shirt, dark blue jeans and low-slung cowman's boots.

It was the long face beneath his curl-brimmed pale grey hat that commanded Kate's attention most of all, though. It had been burnt to the colour of burnished copper by years of exposure to the sun, and it played host to a long, straight nose and a wide, sober mouth. His eyebrows and sideburns, she noticed, were a shade or two darker than desert sand.

He looked down at her and their eyes locked for just a moment. His were mahogany brown, a little sad and, she thought, strangely cautious. She decided that he was perhaps three or four years her senior.

'This here's my top hand, Gil Singleton,' said Keyes. 'Give me a hand with the luggage, will you, Gil?'

The tall cowboy offered her a nod of greeting and muttered something perfunctory about wishing her a good stay. Kate returned the nod as he headed for the trunk of the Tahoe and started to collect baggage.

For a while, the Keyes' busied themselves greeting their guests and helping to break the ice between them. Then the newcomers were ushered into the house itself, which had been built along simple, utilitarian lines, with sturdy oak floors across which had been thrown colourful Indian rugs. Sunshine streamed in through a mixture of double-hung, picture and sliding windows to make the place warm and inviting.

After checking in, Kate was given directions to her room, which was situated on the first floor. As tempting as the cabins out by the lake had appeared in Meadow Springs' brochure, she had booked a room in the house itself because she had felt it would be more convenient for the job she had been sent here to do.

The room turned out to be bright and spacious, furnished with a wardrobe and chest-of-drawers, a TV and DVD player, and a wide single bed across which had been spread a distinctive log cabin-patterned red and blue quilt.

Flopping down on the edge of the bed, she ran her fingers through her short, dark hair and wished she didn't feel quite so apprehensive. She hadn't felt at all like this before. What lay ahead then had been an adventure, excitement, a chance to prove herself.

But now . . .

She actually jumped when there came a discreet knock at the door. She came up off the bed to answer it, and found Glenn Keyes' top hand, Gil Singleton, standing hipshot in the hallway outside. He was holding her cases.

'Hope I didn't disturb you,' he said. His voice was low and measured.

She shook her head. 'Of course not. Please, come in. You can leave those anywhere.'

He went past her and set the cases down on the bed. He smelled of cedar wood and soap, she thought, but

14

beneath that there was an undeniable ruggedness to him that spoke of hard riding and campfires and a life spent outdoors.

That he was tough and durable was beyond dispute. And yet she couldn't forget the sadness she'd seen in his eyes earlier, which hinted at a sensitive nature, and couldn't help wondering what had caused it.

The chore done, he touched his fingers to his hat brim, said so-long and closed the door softly behind him. Kate looked at the door for a moment, wondering at his taciturn manner. But then her own problems came flooding back to the fore. She was here to do a job of work. A very *serious* job of work.

Deciding to unpack before she did anything else, she opened her suitcase, took out the top layer of clothes — and froze.

Her attention had been taken by another item she had placed in the case, and which she had temporarily forgotten. It nestled against a neatly folded blouse, and it looked small, black and ugly.

It was a .38 calibre revolver.

Setting the clothes in her hands aside, she reached down and hesitantly took hold of the weapon. Although it was surprisingly small and compact, it felt big and heavy in her grasp.

Would she have need of the gun while she was here? And if she *did*, could she actually bring herself to *use* it?

She studied it speculatively, as if the weapon itself would supply her with the answer.

In the very next moment, however, she heard the door click open again and spun around, blue eyes widening in a mixture of surprise, guilt and alarm.

Gil Singleton stood in the doorway.

And his dark eyes were fixed on the gun in her hand.

2

He stared into the weapon's short barrel for a long moment, his face unreadable. Then, at last, he said softly, 'You'd better watch where you're pointing that thing.'

His voice, coming slow and easy, seemed to break whatever spell had been holding her there, and she blinked a few times, as if coming out of a dream. Flustering, she quickly put the gun back into her case. 'Don't you believe in knocking first?' she asked, to change the subject.

'I'm sorry. But I forgot to tell you just now. Mr and Mrs Keyes are having a cook-out this evening, around seven. You're invited.'

She nodded stiffly. 'I'll be there. Thank you.'

His eyes fell to her case again, then came back up to her face. Still his expression gave nothing away. 'See you later, then, I guess,' he said at length. 'Oh, and Miss Kate?'

'Yes?'

'I'll remember that tip about knocking next time.'

He closed the door quietly behind him.

⋆   ⋆   ⋆

When Kate came down later that evening, the cook-out was already underway in the unfenced back yard.

Trestle tables covered in blue gingham were covered with bowls of fruit, vegetables, salad and potato chips. A small refrigeration unit had been well stocked with sodas. As befitted the host, Glenn Keyes was busy at a charcoal grill at the far end of the yard, cooking capon breasts and legs, steaks, cauliflower florets and potatoes in tinfoil pouches.

Lamps had been strung everywhere against the coming dusk, and they threw a cosy yellow glow across the people, both visitors and cow-hands, who were cheerfully getting to know each other beneath them. A catchy country-and-western ballad was issuing from speakers which had also been set up around the area.

Kate had no sooner paused on the fringe of the gathering than someone took her by the arm and she turned to find Glenn Keyes's wife, Blanche, smiling at her.

'Now, let me see,' said the woman, 'You must be Kate. Glenn told me all about the charming young girl he'd met this afternoon.'

Kate returned the smile. 'Well, I'm not sure if charming is the word *I'd* use, but you're right, I'm Kate.'

'Well, I'm Blanche, so now we aren't strangers any more. Come on, honey, let's get you a drink.'

She was a still-attractive woman in her late forties, a little above average height and trim-figured, with short, loose brown hair and lively, intelligent hazel eyes. She was dressed casually in a short-sleeved, cream-coloured blouse worn over light brown corduroy pants.

She led Kate to the refrigerator and poured her a glass of green-tomato juice which, as it turned out, tasted much better than it actually sounded.

'I don't seem to recall exactly where you came from,' said Blanche, pulling the tab on a soda she'd chosen for herself.

'Lakedale,' replied Kate, naming a suburb of Denver.

'And you're here all by yourself?'

'Yes. I'm looking forward to a nice, relaxing time.'

'Well, I'm not sure just how relaxing it'll be. We have quite a bit to see and do here at Meadow Spring, you know, maybe even *too* much. We're a working ranch, have been since the late nineteenth century, and we encourage our guests to pitch in and do as much — or as little — as they feel like. But if nursing cows isn't to your taste, we also have an overnight trek to Medwell

— that's a ghost town up in the hills. It takes in some old mine workings and even a prehistoric Indian burial site that has to be seen to be believed.'

'It sounds very tempting, I must admit.'

'Oh, you're going to love it,' Blanche predicted. She glanced around as she took a sip of her soda, her attention lingering briefly on Gil Singleton, who was standing on the far edge of the crowd, nursing a beer and looking distinctly ill-at-ease. 'You've met Gil, I take it?' she said.

'Yes.'

'What did you think?'

'Well, he certainly looks like a cowboy.'

'He should do. His father and grandfather before him both worked at Meadow Spring. Cowboying is the only thing Gil knows.' Blanche's attention was suddenly taken by a movement to her left, and she said, 'Have you met John and Maureen Kelton?'

She put one hand on Kate's arm and

turned her toward the elderly couple she had noticed earlier. Introductions were made, during which John Kelton, a cheerful, heavily-set seventy-year-old with thin, snow-white hair, spoke enthusiastically about all the trout fishing he was hoping to do over the next week or so.

'We're regulars here at Meadow Spring,' his wife explained. 'We just love the place. These folks, the atmosphere . . . you just can't get that homely feel anywhere else.'

'Well, we do *try*, Maureen,' Blanche laughed. 'Though I have to admit, it's folks like you who *really* make it like home.'

They chatted for a while, having to raise their voices to be heard above the music. Whenever Kate was asked about herself, however, she kept her answers vague and quickly changed the subject.

Some time later, Blanche led her towards the grill, saying, 'You really must try some of Glenn's *frico caldo*.'

'What on earth is that?'

'It's a blend of potatoes, cheese and onions. Mexican, of course. You'll love it!'

Blanche filled a plate for her and added some salad, then excused herself, pleading duties elsewhere.

The food was delicious, but Kate was too preoccupied to really enjoy it. The doubts had come creeping back in, this time with a vengeance. After all, what did she *really* know about being a field operator? How could she have even *considered* volunteering for it? Why *had* she, anyway? *Doug?*

The name brought her up sharp.

She'd tried to put him out of her mind. *Tried* to. But stubbornly he refused to go, and she had no clear idea why. It wasn't even as if she still had feelings for him. She *didn't*. No: more likely it was the manner of their parting that still haunted her . . .

For the next hour or so she kept to the fringes of the gathering, watching as a couple of cow-hands, including Randall Woodward, joined Dan and Joe in a game of softball. But now that he had come back into her mind, memories of Doug only added to her woes.

'How're you doing, little missy?'

Glenn Keyes, his face still red from cooking, had left the grill to circulate. Now he studied her with his thumbs hooked into the pockets of his tan leather vest. 'You got enough to eat there? 'Cause there's plenty to go around.'

'More than enough, thank you,' she assured him. 'No, I was just thinking. On a night like this, it's easy to pretend you've travelled back in time, and that this really *is* the Old West of yesterday.'

He nodded agreement. 'That feeling never leaves me,' he confessed. 'And neither would I want it to. Seems to me that the more civilized we get, the more complicated things become. I'll take those old days any time. They were a darn sight simpler.'

'But a whole lot more violent,' she pointed out.

He eyed her askance. 'Aw, you don't

want to believe all the hooey you read in those cowboy books. Things might have been rough, but they weren't all that violent.'

'But they had more than their share of trouble in those days, didn't they?' she persisted. 'Outlaws. Rustlers.'

A nerve ticked in his right cheek, just below the eye, or maybe it was just a trick of the light. 'I think you've been watching too many John Wayne movies,' he opined. 'Now, if you'll excuse me . . . '

He went off to slap backs and crack jokes, and Kate had to confess that he was very, very good at it. But she, too, had work to do.

Whilst checking in, she had fixed the position of Keyes' office firmly in her mind. It had seemed to be the best place for her to begin the work she had been sent here to do.

Casually, she edged back toward the house. As near as she could tell, no-one seemed to notice her go. She disappeared inside and hurried through the large family room, with its chunky, rustic furniture and enormous plasma-screen TV, then on into the unlit hallway beyond. It was here, from behind an oak-panelled door set into the left-side wall, that Keyes operated the ranch.

Holding her breath, she reached for the handle and turned it. As she'd expected, the door was locked. But if she was to believe what she'd been told, that was no problem. The so-called 'bump key' in her pants pocket would soon open it.

She was just reaching for the key when a voice, coming low and start-lingly close beside her, said, 'You got a problem here, Miss Kate?'

'Uh — !'

She spun, unable to stop the soft cry of surprise that spilled from her lips, and in almost the same moment she became aware of that distinctive mix-ture of cedar wood and soap again, and realised that it was Gil Singleton who was crowding her there in the gloom, though how he had come upon her so quietly she had no idea.

Her reaction froze him where he stood, a big, black silhouette facing her from a distance of no more than two or three feet.

'Sorry if I startled you,' he said, though he didn't sound especially sorry at all. 'It's just that I heard a sound in here, figured it was someone sneaking around — '

Although her heart was still hammering, she recovered herself enough to say, 'You often have people sneaking around after dark in these parts, do you?'

He inclined one shoulder. 'It's been known.'

'Oh?'

She was hoping he might say more on the subject, but he didn't. 'Well, like I said, I'm sorry,' was his only response. 'Walk you back to the party?'

'That's all right. I . . . I can find my own way.'

'Fair enough.'

He waited until she had gone past him before he said, 'Ah, Miss Kate?'

She turned back. 'Yes?'

'What were you looking for, anyway?'

She looked blank. 'L-looking for?'

'Around here?' he asked.

She made a vague gesture with one hand. 'Oh, I . . . I've got a headache. All that travelling, I guess. I was, ah, looking for a restroom.'

It sounded pretty weak, even to *her*, but he let it pass. 'Well, I won't detain you. But don't stray too far. The best part of the cook-out's still to come.'

'Really?'

He nodded. 'Mrs Keyes makes a pretty neat hot chocolate. She tops it with coconut cream. It's kind of hard to beat.'

She nodded, turned and left on legs that still felt jittery.

★   ★   ★

Kate woke early next morning to the smells of frying bacon and toasting

28

bread. She threw back the covers and headed for the *en suite* shower, determined to make the day count and do what she could to make headway.

Breakfast tasted as good as it smelled, and she ate well. Owners and guests ate together, and the atmosphere around the long, gingham-covered table was warm and familiar. John Kelton told everyone he was going to spend the day fishing, and wouldn't quit until he'd caught the largest trout at Meadow Spring. His wife joked that they shouldn't expect to see him again for several days.

There was no set itinerary at the ranch. Guests were as free to pursue organized activities as they were to simply please themselves. When Glenn Keyes singled Kate out, she said she wanted to take a ride and see something of the land itself.

'I'll get one of the men to accompany you,' he offered.

'That's okay,' Kate replied hurriedly. 'I'll be fine on my own.'

But Blanche Keyes wasn't so sure. 'That's a lot of country out there, honey. I'd hate for you to get lost.'

'I'll risk it.'

'Just stick to the trails,' said Keyes, 'and you should be fine.'

After breakfast, and while Blanche arranged a packed lunch for her, Kate went up to her room to get her baseball cap and sunglasses. She'd left the cap hanging from a hook on the back of the door, the glasses on the chest-of-drawers. Or *had* she? When she looked, there was no sign of the glasses.

Frowning, because she was almost certain she'd left the glasses there shortly after arriving the previous afternoon, she made a quick search of the room and found them on the window shelf instead. She'd obviously made a mistake.

Planting the baseball cap on her head, she went to the door, but hesitated with her hand on the knob and, impulsively, subjected the room to a more careful scrutiny. Everything looked exactly as she remembered it, and yet she had the uncomfortable feeling that the room had been searched in her absence.

As the suspicion began to turn into a certainty, she went to the wardrobe, took out her case, set it down on the floor, flicked the catches and opened the lid.

Hurriedly she rifled through her clothes. Nothing appeared to have been touched, but . . .

Suddenly her sharp intake of breath was the only sound.

But the gun had gone!

A cold tingle washed through her. She'd been right, then. Someone *had* gone through her things!

But who — and *why?* Gil Singleton had seen the gun. He must have wondered about it. He might even have been afraid that she would cause injury with it, not least to herself.

But would he have taken it upon himself to steal the weapon away from her? She doubted it. He'd have spoken to her about it . . . *wouldn't* he?

Wouldn't he?

She didn't like the doubts that began creeping into her mind.

Putting the case back, she left the room and went back downstairs, where she collected her packed lunch and then went outside.

She found Randall Woodward at one of the barns, exercising quarter-horses in an adjoining corral. His smile broadened when he saw her, but it was a predatory smile that left her feeling distinctly uncomfortable.

'Well, well, and a good morning to you!' he greeted. 'What brings you over to see little ol' me?'

'I'm going for a ride,' she replied. 'I was told you could fit me out with a horse.'

'Sure can. You done any riding before?'

'Once or twice. Not much.'

'I'll give you an older horse, then,' he decided. 'Come on, I'll show you how to saddle up.'

He made it look easy, and did it all so deliberately fast that she couldn't follow it at all. It might have been her imagination, but she was sure he had also selected the biggest and most powerful-looking horse he could find.

At last he handed her the split reins and said, 'He's all yours. Have a good ride, and if any part of you needs rubbing in with liniment later, you just come straight to *me*, got it?'

Uncomfortably aware of her own limitations as a rider, and the fact that he was scrutinizing her closely, she toed into the stirrup, took firm hold of the saddle horn and mounted up. Once settled, she cautiously walked the horse out into the pleasant morning sunshine. That, however, was as far as she got.

The horse immediately began to give her problems. It kept baulking and refusing to move. Woodward, leaning against the door-frame and crossing his arms, enquired lightly, 'Having trouble there, ma'am?'

She struggled to keep the horse from

turning, but the animal paid her no mind. Behind her, she heard Woodward call, 'Like for me to give you a couple of riding lessons first, Miss Kate?'

By now another two cowboys had been drawn by all the commotion. Kate could only guess at what they were thinking: that here was a silly city girl who couldn't even make an apparently docile horse go where she wanted it to. And just to make things worse, Gil Singleton came out of the bunkhouse at just that moment to witness her struggles for himself.

After another moment he strode over, grabbed the reins and took hold of the horse's big jaw. At once the restless animal calmed, and despite herself, Kate was both surprised and impressed by the top hand's obvious way with animals.

'Step down a minute, ma'am,' he said.

Slowly, she did just that.

When she was standing beside him, he reached down and unbuckled the cinch-strap beneath the horse's belly, then gave the saddle itself a shove, so that it slipped from the horse's back and fell to the ground. When he peeled back the saddle blanket, she saw that something small had stuck in the horse's glistening coat.

'It is a teasel burr,' murmured Gil. It was a small seed covered in tiny hooks, which would easily attach itself to you should you brush against it in the wild. He carefully removed it from the horse's back.

'Who saddled up for you, ma'am?' he asked.

Kate was about to reply, then thought better of it. She'd never been the type to tell on anyone. But a brief movement of her eyes toward Randall Woodward betrayed her. Gil turned and called, 'Better come and re-saddle this animal properly, Randy.'

Woodward glanced from left to right, at his snickering companions, his soft, round face a picture of injured innocence. 'What's that supposed to mean?' he demanded. 'I saddled it properly the *first* time.'

'You put a burr under the blanket so the horse would cause problems,' Gil replied, biting out the words. 'Well, okay, you've had your fun. But do it again, and you're fired.'

Woodward looked as if he'd been slapped. 'Hey now, listen here! I didn't plant that burr, and there's nothing to say I did!'

Despite the other man's threatening manner, Gil stood his ground. 'I don't need proof where you're concerned, Woodward. I know you of old. Now saddle up, and this time do it *right.*'

The order given, Gil turned back to Kate, looking uncomfortable. 'Seems all I do when I'm around you is apologise. But what else can I say except sorry?'

Struck by his very genuine concern, she offered him a smile of appreciation. 'No harm done, except maybe to my pride. But thank you for coming to my rescue.'

His eyebrows met in a brief frown. 'I

was more concerned about the horse,' he said without thinking.

His statement rocked her back on her heels, and whatever emotions she'd allowed to thaw for this man suddenly iced up again. 'Well, thank you for coming to the *horse's* rescue, then,' she said tartly.

Only then did he seem to realise what he'd said, and how it'd sounded. 'Aw,' he muttered as she turned away and marched back toward the horse. 'I didn't mean to say — '

But it was too late. She'd already gathered her reins, stepped into the saddle and left the yard without a backward glance.

★   ★   ★

As the ranch fell behind her and the valley opened up ahead, Kate told herself that she had been silly to react the way she'd had. After all, what was so wrong in putting the horse's welfare first? And what did it matter to her if he was more concerned about the horse than its rider?

It shouldn't matter a bit. And yet, confusingly, it seemed to matter quite a lot.

She shook her head. She was getting distracted, and that was something she mustn't allow. Heeling the horse to a long trot, she followed the trail across a great open expanse of prairie covered in yellow, just-blooming scurfpea. Ahead lay a modest fringing of juniper, beyond which chocolate-coloured slopes led up to a series of sky-scraping peaks and crags. Here and there, cattle grazed contentedly, so used to the presence of humans that few even bothered to give her a second look.

She reined down and helped herself to a sip of water from her canteen. For the first time she understood just how the problem she had been sent here to investigate could prove to be so seemingly insoluble.

The day wore one. She had no idea how many miles she covered, but it was an awful lot. By noon she was following a dried-up watercourse that snaked this way and that through high rock walls. It eventually led out to a gentle, rock-littered slope above which lay lush tableland.

Ascending the slope, she eventually happened upon a pleasant, thin stream, where she decided to stop for the lunch Blanche Keyes' cook had packed. She allowed the horse to drink from the stream first, then sat in tree-shade, enjoying the peace and isolation of the spot. It was a good place to think without interruption.

Not that it did her much good. She was still at the beginning of her quest, and so far had precious little information upon which to base her thinking.

It was just as she was packing away and getting ready to move on again that she had the strongest feeling she was being watched.

At first she tried to tell herself that it was just her imagination. She wasn't used to these wide open spaces, and understood that they could easily have such an effect. From behind her sunglasses she surveyed her surroundings. The country was uneven, with a number of dips and ridges behind which someone could watch her without being seen.

Again she thought about the missing gun, the fact that her room had been searched. She didn't like to think what it might mean — or how vulnerable she suddenly felt.

Willing herself not to panic — knowing it could be potentially fatal if she did — she finished packing and remounted. She pointed the horse back the way she'd come and began to descend the shale-covered slope again.

Horse and rider were about half-way down when there came a sudden, spiteful snapping sound, and the horse reared up with a startled whinny. Taken by surprise, Kate felt herself falling backwards out of the saddle. The world became a crazy kaleidoscope of ground and sky: then she landed hard with a clatter, and the breath left her in a rush.

She had just enough time for one painful moan, then remembered the horse. She opened her eyes again just in time to see the animal following the lines of the dried watercourse around a bend.

Kate knew a fleeting moment of despair, but that was quickly shoved aside when she remembered what had caused the horse to bolt in the first place. That sharp, spiteful snapping sound.

The sound of a gunshot!

Even as she realized what had happened, she began moving, half-running, half-scuttling for the cover of a nearby cluster of rocks. She flung herself down behind them, the sawing of her quick, frightened breathing loud in her ears.

And then came that thought, that dreadful, terrifying thought.

Someone's trying to kill me! Someone is actually trying to kill me!

3

Somehow an hour passed. It was a long, hot, dry, tension-filled hour. But she neither saw nor heard anything else to suggest that her hidden assailant — assuming there had been an assailant to *begin* with — was still out there.

She sighed, feeling thoroughly discouraged. The sun was slowly sliding toward the west, she was aching, scared and set afoot in the middle of nowhere. Even if she broke cover now and started retracing her steps — and that was a big *if*, because she had long-since realized that she had no idea in just which direction she would find the ranch — it would soon be too dark, and thus too dangerous, to travel.

Her spirits dropped even lower. But she couldn't stay here all night. And maybe, if she was lucky, her horse wouldn't have gone too far.

She gave her surroundings one more thorough scrunity, but was as convinced as she could be that she was now all alone. Taking a deep breath, she finally straightened out of her long-held crouch —

— and gave a small cry.

She must have twisted her ankle as well as her neck when she fell from the horse. Now a sharp, stabbing pain shot through her right leg and she almost collapsed again.

So much for trying to *walk* anywhere.

Despair flooded back in, but this time there was a flare of anger as well, a sense of indignation that chased away her fear and made her more determined than ever to carry out the job which had brought her here in the first place.

It was about then that a sound reached her from the watercourse below. *Someone was coming this way!* But who was it — friend or foe?

Her brief moment of excitement quickly turned to caution. She strained to see the trail below the rocks, but it was empty. Still, whoever was down there was coming closer. The sound of horse hooves on stone was growing louder.

Dare she risk calling for help? Perhaps she should wait until the newcomer had shown himself, then decide —

But then all thought was interrupted by a new sound, coming from behind her.

She thought, *Oh, no* . . .

It was the unmistakable rattle of a snake.

★   ★   ★

Just when she thought things couldn't get worse, it seemed that they had.

When she turned her head, she saw just how bad they were.

Barely six feet away, a long, slim snake was staring at her, its tail vibrating so fast that it was almost impossible to see. She had disturbed the creature from its slumber when she'd fallen after trying to stand up, and now it was angry.

The snake was black, but its every shiny scale was speckled with flecks of yellow and white. Under other circumstances she would have appreciated its beauty, but just then all she could think of was its staring eyes, its split, flickering tongue, its willingness to bite as it uncoiled and slid slowly closer.

It was, she thought, about four feet long.

She heard a soft sound that made her jump. It was a moment before she realized that it was a low moan, and that it had come from her own tight throat.

The snake edged a little nearer, still fixing her with its black, unblinking eyes. Behind her, and somewhere below, the clattering hoof beats had grown louder, then stopped. She wanted to turn her head to see what was happening below, but somehow her head refused to move. She just couldn't take her eyes off --

The snake slid closer, its long body coiling and flexing behind its flat expressionless head. No more than three feet separated them now. One more push and the snake would be close enough to rear up and lunge at her face —

It was then that Kate sensed a sudden movement off to her left. She heard crunching footfalls coming unhurriedly toward her. A shadow fell across her, then moved on.

In the next moment *he* was there, Gil Singleton, and he was bending to one knee beside the snake.

She didn't see his hand move, but it must have, because in the blink of an eye his right hand was gripping the snake behind the head, and as it began to writhe furiously, he took hold of its body with his left and picked it up.

As she watched, he carried the snake a few yards away, then gently set it down in the cool shade of some rocks. As the reptile slithered away, he came back over to her, looking big, capable,

46

and just a little irritated.

'You've caused quite a stir back at the ranch,' he said by way of greeting. 'When your horse came in all by himself . . . '

Her mouth opened and closed a few times before she finally found her voice. 'You c-came out to find me?'

'Mr Keyes sent me,' he said. 'I guess he was afraid you might've had an accident.' He looked down at her with his thumbs hooked into his belt. 'Looks like he was right. What happened? You take a fall?'

She hesitated before replying, and for a moment studied him covertly from beneath her fringe. Was he genuinely concerned, or just surprised that his shot — if he was the one who had fired it — had failed to find its target?

'Uh, yes.'

She didn't want to tell anyone that she'd been shot at, at least not yet. And to be truthful, she still wasn't completely sure that she *had* been shot at.

'Thank you for coming to find me.

And for the way you handled that snake just now,' she told him, unable to resist adding, 'Or was it that you were thinking more of the snake's welfare than mine?'

A half-smile tugged briefly at his mouth. 'You're not going to let me forget that, are you?' he said, dropping to his haunches before her. 'Snake weren't no threat, but I guess he gave you a turn.'

'It was rattling its tail at me.'

'They do that, when you put 'em on the defensive. But them kingsnakes, they prefer just to go about their business and let you do the same.'

'And I suppose I've taken you away from *your* business?'

'I'm not complaining. Sometimes it's nice to get away from the ranch, just ride, breathe the good, clean air and see the scenery.' Abruptly the frown came back to his brow. 'You hurt?' he asked.

'I twisted my neck and ankle. That's about it.'

He indicated the trail below with a

nod of his head. Two horses stood patiently at the edge of the watercourse, their reins hanging loose to the ground ahead of them, to stop them from wandering.

'I brought a spare horse. Think you can ride back? Without taking another fall, I mean.'

'If you'll help me down off this slope.'

'Sure.'

His touch was light, strong and surprisingly gentle. He took her arm and helped her back to her feet, but it hurt to put weight on her twisted ankle and she stumbled forward against his chest. He took her weight easily, scooping her into his arms and slowly picking his way back down the slope, carrying her as if she were a child.

'Better get some ice on that ankle when we get back, have Mrs Keyes check it out, make sure it's just a sprain and nothing much else.'

'I'm sure it'll be okay,' she said.

He inclined one shoulder in a sort of

half-shrug. 'I guess. But you should never underestimate an injury.'

'You sound as if you're talking from experience.'

He gave a short, humourless laugh, 'I am.'

When they reached the horses, he gently set her down and then helped her mount the spare animal. When she was safely astride, he climbed into his own saddle and got them moving back in the general direction of the ranch. Kate noticed that he deliberately kept the pace slow so as not to aggravate her injuries any more than was necessary, and appreciated it.

The slanting sun warmed their backs and sent their shadows questing out ahead of them. In the distance, small bunches of cattle clustered together, mostly black but with some reds mixed in with them, some with splashes of white around their udders, all of them hornless.

'They're Angus cattle, aren't they?' said Kate.

He nodded. 'Yes'm. They mature fast, breed well and they give plenty of good meat. They're kind of docile, too, so they're a sight easier to handle than some breeds I've known.'

'You're talking from experience again.'

'Uh-huh.' He fell silent a moment, then asked, 'How'd it happen?'

She glanced over at him. 'How did *what* happen?'

'How you came to fall off your horse.'

She flustered and tried to hide the fact. 'Oh, he . . . he spooked. I couldn't say why. He just reared up and threw me.'

'You're lucky you didn't break your neck.'

Maybe that was the idea, she thought with a sudden flash of insight. If someone had discovered her true purpose here and wanted to get rid of her . . . well, who could argue with an accident? No wonder she'd just assumed that the bullet had missed its target. It was far more likely that they were trying to get rid of her in a less obvious fashion — whoever *they* were.

With the revelation came another concern. Her cover, such as it was, had been blown, exposing her for exactly what she was. But how? There had to be a leak somewhere . . .

Again she heard Gil's last sentence in her mind. This time it made her shudder.

You're lucky you didn't break your neck.

* * *

Despite her misgivings, Kate was welcomed back to the ranch like a long-lost family member. Blanche Keyes gave her a hug and helped her upstairs to her room, where she made a quick inspection of Kate's injuries. Satisfied that there was nothing a good rest wouldn't cure, she left Kate to take a shower.

'Would you prefer to take supper in

your room tonight?' she asked solici-
tously, at the door.

'No, I'll be fine.'

'Good. Mr Kelton's celebrating his
good fortune with champagne tonight,
and I know he'd like you to be there to
share his moment of glory.'

Kate thought for a moment. 'You
don't mean to say that he actually *did*
catch the biggest trout in Meadow
Spring?'

Blanche chuckled. 'Well maybe not
the *biggest*, but quite a monster.'

'I'll be there.'

When she was left alone, Kate
grabbed a towel and hobbled into the
shower. As she had hoped, the hot
water chased some of the aches and
pains away. Afterwards, feeling a little
better, she went to the wardrobe and
took out her case, deciding to wear a
plaid blouse and a denim skirt for the
evening meal.

As soon as she lifted the lid of the
case, however, she realized that someone had been through her belongings

again. There was just *something* about the way everything had been re-arranged . . .

Quickly now she rummaged through the contents to see what else had been taken. But *nothing* had been taken.

On the contrary, something had been put *back*.

The gun!

4

Kate slept fitfully that night, and not just because of her injuries. She had come to Meadow Spring for a specific purpose. But so far she'd seemed to be getting nowhere fast.

Should she concede defeat, go back to Denver with her tail between her legs?

No. It was too soon for that. And what would she achieve by quitting, except to confirm that she was, after all, one of life's losers?

She rose early the following morning, enjoyed a light breakfast and then sat out on the front patio, pretending to read a magazine, but in reality trying to decide upon some strategy that might change her luck and yield results.

She was just going back indoors, intending to try and sneak a more successful look around Glenn Keyes' office, when she ran into two people coming from the opposite direction. It was John and Maureen Kelton, who were both looking somewhat animated.

'Hello, Kate,' greeted Kelton. 'Where are you off to in such a hurry?'

'Oh, nowhere special.'

'Aren't you coming over to the corral to watch the show?'

She frowned. 'Show?'

He nodded keenly. 'The foreman, Gil Singleton. He's going to break a horse to the saddle.'

'Not *break*,' corrected his long-suffering wife. 'The term is *gentle*. He's going to *gentle* a horse that's never been ridden before, and Glenn Keyes says he's going to do it in less than twenty minutes.'

'I say it can't be done,' declared Kelton. 'In fact, I've even made a small wager on it.'

'A *not-so* small wager,' laughed his wife.

'Glenn Keyes stands to receive a very handsome windfall if Gil Singleton proves him wrong.'

'Which he won't,' Kelton said with certainty.

'Well, whether he does or he doesn't, it's certainly going to be something to see,' decided Maureen. 'So — are you coming over?'

Kate's immediate instinct was to say no, and make the most of the distraction in order to attempt another search of Glenn Keyes' office.

But it quickly became obvious that the Keltons wouldn't take no for an answer.

'All right,' she said at length. 'You win.'

She followed the elderly couple across the yard to one of the two corrals, around which a mixture of guests and ranch hands had gathered under the watchful eye of Glenn and Blanche Keyes, who were standing on a small dais. When Glenn was satisfied that everyone was assembled, he raised his voice.

'Now, what we're going to do here

this morning is take a yearling that's never before known the weight of a saddle on his back, much less the weight of a *rider*, and turn him into a darn fine riding horse in about twenty minutes,' he announced. 'There are some folks — mentioning no names, Mr Kelton — ' and here he paused while laughter rippled through his audience, ' — there are *some* folks who say it can't be done, and certainly not without ill-treating the horse concerned.

'Well, here at Meadow Spring we think that's just so much hooey. We're not in the business of *breaking* animals, we *gentle* them. That is to say, our *foreman*, Gil Singleton, gentles them. No ill-treatment, no threats, no punishment. What you're about to see now is truly something.'

He glanced at his wife, who was holding a stopwatch in her left hand. 'Ready, Blanche?'

'Ready!'

'Okay, Gil. On your marks . . . get set . . . *GO!*'

Kate's heart skipped a beat when Gil came out of the large adjoining barn and led a young, uncertain-looking quarter-horse into the corral. The crowd fell silent as Gil let go of the horse's bridle and allowed it to trot to the far side of the enclosure.

In his free hand, Gil had been holding a length of coiled rope. Now he flicked it loose and sent the free end skittering out to catch the horse lightly behind its rear hooves. In this way, he kept the horse trotting around the corral, first one way for perhaps five laps, then the other for the same amount.

'Notice the horse's ears,' called Keyes. 'See how they're angled toward Gil?'

At last Gil re-coiled the rope and tossed it aside. The horse stopped trotting and eyed him cautiously. Gil walked slowly over to the animal, taking a meandering route and never once looking the animal in the eye. In fact, Kate saw, he made a point to keep his head half-turned away from the yearling at all times.

Then, almost before the horse realized it, Gil had taken hold of the bridle and was rubbing the animal's long muzzle affectionately. The horse wasn't too sure how to react, so he just stood there and allowed Gil to continue.

'Six minutes,' called Blanche.

It was then that an amazing thing happened.

Gil turned his back on the horse and walked away from it . . . and the horse, without a second's hesitation, went after him, constantly nudging his shoulder to get his attention.

Gil went back into the barn and reappeared a few moments later carrying a saddle and blanket. He set them down on the ground and waited patiently while the horse, still curious, came back to him and gingerly sniffed at the items at Gil's feet.

'Nine minutes,' called Blanche.

Still apparently ignoring the horse.

Gil made one circuit of the corral, then came back to the saddle and blanket. The horse, now utterly devoted to him, shadowed him every step of the way.

This time, Gil picked up the blanket and appeared to examine it. Again the horse sniffed it.

Gil rubbed the blanket along the horse's muzzle, between its large, shiny eyes. Then, without breaking stride, he threw the blanket across the horse's back. The horse side-stepped a little, then, at Gil's soft, gentle urging, settled back down.

'Ten minutes.'

Still not hurrying, Gil bent and picked up the saddle. The horse eyed him worriedly. Gil carefully lifted the saddle and settled it onto the blanket, leaving it unfastened. For now, it seemed to be enough just to let the horse get used to the unaccustomed weight.

'Twelve minutes.'

Kate, only half-aware of Blanche's voice, continued to watch Gil in complete fascination.

'This here's the crucial part,' called Glenn Keyes. 'When Gil actually buckles the saddle *on*.'

Carefully, Gil took hold of the cinch-strap and let it down. Then he walked around to the horse's off-side, pulled the strap beneath the horse's belly and buckled it tight. Once again the yearling side-stepped nervously, but the explosive reaction of sound and movement that everyone was expecting failed to materialize.

Instead, Gil went back to his coiled rope, allowed it to fall loose and once again used it to make the horse lap the corral at a trot, first one way for about five circuits, then the other.

'Sixteen minutes,' called Blanche.

The horse slowed to a stop and Gil tossed the rope aside. He walked straight up to the horse and took the reins in one hand and the saddle horn in the other. Instead of mounting up, however, he simply hoisted himself across the saddle, so that his legs were hanging one side, his head, arms and torso the other.

'Eighteen minutes.'

Beside her, John Kelton chuckled, and Kate heard him mutter to his wife, 'Told you he couldn't do it in twenty minutes. This is going to be the easiest hundred dollars I ever won.'

The horse walked a few steps with Gil's weight on him, not really sure what was expected of him. After a while, Gil slipped back to the ground and rubbed the horse's head again.

Blanche Keyes called out, 'Nineteen minutes,' and Kate heard John Kelton murmur, 'Like taking candy from a baby.'

But the smile left his face when Gil suddenly stepped into the stirrup and this time, mounted correctly. The horse froze momentarily, then Gil touched his heels lightly against the animal's sides and it began to trot around the corral as if it had been a trained saddle-horse for as long as it could remember.

It was a magnificent, almost touching

sight, and Kate was surprised when she had to stop applauding and brush a tear from her eye.

'That'll be a hundred dollars, if you please, Mr Kelton!' Glenn Keyes called down with a grin.

Kelton looked shamed-faced as he called back, 'Do you take American Express?'

Everyone laughed.

The demonstration over and the horse relaxing by the moment as it grew ever more used to being ridden, Gil reined down, dismounted and treated the animal to an expressive show of affection and praise. As far as Kate was concerned, watching him with the horse was like watching a completely different man.

Gone was Gil's near-constant scowl. He was relaxed now, and in repose he looked younger, happier, a man in his true element.

Then he happened to look up and saw her watching him as everyone else drifted away from the corral, and all at once he looked painfully self-conscious. The smile left his face and the scowl came back. He led the horse back into the barn and out of sight.

'I'll say one thing for him,' said a voice, speaking suddenly from behind her, 'he knows horses better than any man I've ever met.'

She turned to find Randall Woodward looking down at her. 'Mr Keyes tells me I've got a calf and his mama to fetch in from Bluebird Canyon,' he said. 'Thought you might care to go along for the ride.'

She offered him a cool, quizzical look. 'And what makes you think I'd like to do that?'

''Cause I'd like to say sorry for that stunt I pulled yesterday,' he replied. 'And I think it would do you good. After all, what's the thing they always tell you to do when you get thrown from a horse?'

'Get right back on,' she answered thoughtfully. He had a point. And just maybe he was genuine in his desire to make amends for the previous morning. 'All right. Thank you.'

He smiled briefly. 'I'll go saddle the horses. Shouldn't take us long to haze them cows back in. Calf'll follow his mama anywhere we push her.'

He was gone for just as long as it took him to prepare two horses for riding, but as he led them out of the barn, Glenn Keyes appeared on the patio and called his name. Leaving the horses ground-hitched, he went over to see what his boss wanted, then came back a few minutes later, the disappointment in his face plain to see.

'Sorry, Miss Kate. The boss's found me some other chores to tend to. But you could always bring those dogies in by yourself.'

'*Me?*' she asked, startled.

'Sure. Blackbird Canyon's only about three miles that-a-way. The cattle are docile enough, they'll just go where you tell them to.'

She chewed at her lower lip. 'I hope this isn't another one of your *jokes.*'

'No, ma'am, 'Fact, it was Mr Keyes himself who suggested it.'

She let her breath go in a sigh. 'All right,' she replied, taking up the reins of the nearest horse. She couldn't say she was exactly looking forward to the prospect, but he certainly seemed to be sincere, and there was always the chance that she might actually enjoy the experience. 'But you owe me one,' she added with mock severity.

He smiled at her again. 'Thank you, Miss Kate. Just you concentrate on the mama, push her back towards the ranch and the calf will come right after her.'

Gil Singleton was currying the quarter-horse in the barn doorway when she rode out. His dark gaze followed her until she was just a speck in the distance, and as he watched, his dark eyes were troubled.

* * *

She found Bluebird Canyon easily enough. It was reached by way of a rocky gap between two steep slopes covered in spindly poplars and brush.

Reining down briefly, she drank in the rugged beauty of the location. The slopes were great sweeping carpets of verdant brush, the deep greens and browns of the foliage stippled with wild flowers, from tamarisk to fleabane, penny cress and a tall, crimson plant she knew to be called Indian Paintbrush.

It was a beautiful, tranquil scene . . . and yet the isolation of it made her shiver. Only three miles from the ranch, and yet it might just as well have been on the far side of the moon.

To make matters worse, she suddenly had the unshakable conviction that she was being watched again.

It was an eerie feeling, but she guessed it was understandable enough, especially to a girl who had always been used to the hustle and bustle of city life.

In any case, she had a job to do, so she heeled the horse forward, through the gap and into the canyon itself.

A rocky, hard-packed trail wound between towering, earth-coloured walls and buttresses that were seamed, weathered and cracked. Here and there juniper projected from clefts in the canyon walls: elsewhere, wherever it could find a foothold, bright yellow rabbitbrush waved gently in the faint breeze.

There was, however, no sign of the cow and calf she had come to find.

Doggedly she continued to follow the canyon's winding contours. The only sound was the lonely clatter of her horse's hooves on the rocky canyon floor.

She had gone perhaps three-quarters of a mile when she came to a rock fall that prevented her from going any further. At some time in the past, some kind of craggy promontory had finally succumbed to the tireless elements and toppled. Now all that remained was an impassable wall of shattered rocks.

Of course, Kate still hadn't found the animals she had been sent to fetch in, and was certain now that they were no longer here for the finding. There was simply no place for them to have hidden, and no other way she could have overlooked them. Perhaps she had found her way to a different canyon.

She turned her horse and began to retrace her steps. Rounding a bend in the trail a few minutes later, however, she spotted something dark up ahead, and with relief told herself that she had finally found the animals she sought.

But in the very next moment, her grip on the reins tightened and her horse drew up, testing the air and turning nervous.

For that was no heifer up ahead. It was a big, dangerous-looking bull with a dark brown coat, a long neck and sharp, deadly horns curving outwards from its head, which was held high. It was a massive creature, easily fifteen hundred pounds.

And when it saw Kate, its head dropped low and it began to paw at the earth, its manner unmistakably threatening.

5

The horse instinctively took a step backward. Unable to think of anything better to do, Kate gave the animal its head.

The bull pawed at the dirt again, starring at girl and horse through baleful eyes. She tried to curb her instinctive wariness. There was no reason for him to charge her, and maybe he would be content with some harmless posturing, just to tell her that this was his domain and that she was trespassing.

Where had he come from anyway? And if this *was* Bluebird Canyon, where were the animals she had been sent to find?

The bull suddenly threw back his head and made a weird, almost human sound, part moan, part cough, part bellow. But its meaning was clear.

In the next moment he threw himself forward in a lumbering charge, and Kate yanked on the reins to make the horse turn and gallop back the way they had just come. The horse, as scared as her now, needed no second urging.

She hazarded a brief backwards glance. The bull was coming for them with its nostrils flared and its beady eyes opened wide. She had hoped it would be satisfied with a few harmless feints, but didn't hold out much hope.

Then the horse's legs went stiff, dust and dirt exploding up around its hooves, and when she faced front again her eyes widened in horror.

Of course — the rock fall! There would be no escape this way!

She turned the horse again, but this time it was a struggle because the animal was terrified and starting to fight her all the way.

Finally the horse moved, blurred away to the left and made a desperate attempt to scale the far wall. The grade was too steep, though, and he slid back down in a shower of disturbed rocks and dirt, panicking even more.

The bull, meanwhile, had slithered to a halt and turned to follow her every movement. He looked furious as he dug his fore-hooves into the earth, then lowered his big head in preparation for another charge.

By the time he started moving again, Kate had heeled the horse to a gallop and the two of them were surging back along the canyon floor, heading for the only exit.

The bull moved with astonishing speed for its size. A glance back over her shoulder showed Kate that it was no more than ten yards behind her. In the heat of the moment, however, he looked much, much nearer.

Beneath her the horse gave a sickening lurch. The animal had lost its footing in the loose rock and stumbled. Though it managed to recover almost immediately, it lost vital ground, and all at once the bull had halved the distance between them, and Kate knew that one swipe of those razor-sharp horns would cause injury or worse, maybe for them both.

The horse, sensing the nearness of their pursuer, suddenly made a desperate scramble up the brush-choked bank that led up to the sheer canyon wall. They gained just enough height for the bull to cannon on past them, before slipping down again.

But it was only a temporary reprieve. Momentum carried the bull on for several yards. Then he turned again, threw back his head and let go a terrific bawl. A second later his fore-hooves lifted off the ground and a mighty thrust of his hindquarters sent him surging back in Kate's direction.

Without warning, however, a new-comer now entered the fray: a second rider whose chestnut horse came clattering along the canyon floor from the direction of the gap between the hills, a tall, lean man spinning a coil of rope above his head, the other end of which was firmly tied around his saddle horn.

Gil Singleton!

In less time than it took to tell, he came up alongside the charging bull, so close that Kate felt sure the animal would turn its head and gore him.

A split second later, Gil threw the free end of the lariat, the coil into which he had fashioned it dropping neatly over the horns.

Next he turned his horse at a right angle to the bull, stood tall in his stirrups and the horse beneath him came to an abrupt halt.

It took no more than a fraction of a second for the rope around the bull's horns to draw taut. And when it did, the bull was yanked sideways and down onto one side.

The impact left the animal winded, and before he could recover, Gil was throwing himself from the saddle, the other end of the lariat now grasped in his big hands.

As dust rose around him and the bull continued to thresh and try to rise, he quickly threw a loop around each of its fore-hooves, effectively hobbling the animal and restricting its ability to move.

Kate could only watch in astonishment and with a racing heart. Then her surprise turned to concern as Gil staggered away from the bull and, pausing momentarily, put one hand on his left side and cautiously arched his back.

She opened her mouth to call to him, ask if he was okay, but then he seemed to return to his old self and came hurrying over to her.

She began to dismount. As soon as he was near enough he reached up and more or less lifted her from the saddle. As he set her down, they were so close that the buttons on their shirts actually clicked.

He looked down at her, concern plain to see in his gaze, and in that moment the horrors of the last few moments were suddenly forgotten and she was hopelessly loss in his embrace, and blissfully happy to be so.

No words passed between them, and yet an entire conversation seemed to communicate itself in their eyes alone. His grip on her shoulders increased. The pain was close to pleasurable. It was all she could do just to keep breathing.

His expression grew difficult to read. She thought she saw a spark of revelation in him, as if something had suddenly become clear. It left him surprised, apprehensive, confused. And then . . .

And then, his face dropped slowly closer to hers, and her face tilted up to meet it . . .

Behind them, the bull gave an indignant bellow, and though it didn't exactly break the moment, it certainly cracked it, and they both stepped back from one another, pretending that the last few seconds had never happened.

'Are you, uh, all right?' he asked.

She replied with a question of her own. 'I . . . yes, I'm fine. But where did you come from?'

He arched one eyebrow at her. 'Are you complaining?'

'No, of course not, but — '

'I was around,' he said vaguely, 'heard some commotion in here, decided to take a look. Good job I did.'

She nodded. 'You seem to be making a habit out of saving me.'

He looked down at her again, his face very, very serious, and all at once she felt heat flood into her cheeks.

In the next moment his right hand came up and cupped the back of her head, and he drew her to him.

What happened next wasn't so much a kiss as an urgent mashing together of lips, a sudden, startling swelling of desire that was felt as much by Kate as it was by Gil.

His other arm curved around her and pulled her close, and she went willingly. A part of her mind, a small part not completely, utterly consumed by the moment, told her that this could not possibly be happening, that it *shouldn't* be happening, and that she should protest or resist, and yet she wanted only to be carried along with it.

Then the pressure of his lips lessened, albeit reluctantly, and they each drew back, catching their breath now, avoiding each other's eyes.

'I'm sorry, ma'am,' he began.

'You don't have to do that.'

'I *do*,' he insisted. 'I had no right.'

Gradually Kate's breathing calmed. 'I . . . I was glad you came along when you did,' she near-whispered.

He recovered himself, but his discomfort remained obvious. 'What, uh, what happened, anyway?'

Her mind still elsewhere, she told him.

'Sounds to me like another one of Randy's pranks,' he said when she finished.

Anxious not to make a fuss, she told him, 'No harm done — except maybe to the bull.'

Gil threw the creature a quick glance. 'He'll be okay. Heeling him over like that knocked some of the pepper out of him. But this is serious, ma'am. If I hadn't come along . . . '

'But you *did*,' she interrupted. 'Let that be an end to it.'

He eyed her with open curiosity, but made no comment. Instead he told her to remount. 'We'll take this varmint back where he belongs,' he said. 'And then I'm gonna have a few words with Randy Woodward.'

*   *   *

'Come and sit down, Kate,' said Glenn Keyes, looking grave-faced as he ushered her to a chair. 'You just rest up while I pour you a brandy.'

They were in his office, back at the ranch. Gil had delivered her there with a brief explanation of what had happened, then excused himself with a grim look in his eyes.

Now, while Keyes fixed her a drink, Kate made a quick, almost secretive study of her surroundings.

The office was large and bright, with

sturdy pine furniture and leather chairs, the walls hung with a series of canvases depicting various scenes of ranch-life. Her eyes lingered briefly on a locked filing cabinet, and she wondered which of the paintings concealed the wall safe Keyes was bound to have.

Just then he came back and handed her a glass. 'Here,' he said. 'Best thing there is for shock, and that's sure what you must've had.'

'Really,' she replied, 'I'm fine. I just think there was just some kind of . . . misunderstanding.'

He took the chair on the other side of his large desk, where he eyed her with concern. 'That's for sure,' he allowed. 'But misunderstanding or not, I want you to know that we take our responsibilities seriously here, Kate. It's important to us that our guests have a good time, and a *safe* time. Now, you had a bad experience yesterday, and another one today. I wouldn't want you to judge us by that.'

'I wouldn't.'

'Even so,' he went on, 'it could be that the ranching life isn't for you. If that *is* the case, and you think maybe you've made a mistake in choosing this kind of vacation, then I'd be glad to offer you a full refund, and as a gesture of goodwill, and to make up for what's happened, I'll even pay your travel expenses.'

Kate's smiled tiredly. 'That's very generous of you Mr Keyes — '

'*Glenn*.'

She inclined her head. 'Glenn,' she repeated. 'But I didn't expect ranch life to be easy. In any case, I enjoy a challenge, I always have. I'll stay.'

He drew in a breath, not too happy about it but doing his best to hide the fact. 'Well, the offer stands. You change your mind, you just let me know. Meantime, we'll all do whatever we can to make the rest of your time at Meadow Spring unforgettable.'

Kate smiled again. Remembering the touch of Gil Singleton's lips, the earnestness and concern in his eyes, the feel of his muscular arms wrapping gently but insistently around her, she told herself it was *already* unforgettable.

* ★ ★ ★

After supper that evening she went to her room. The events of the day had been a strain, but at the same time she was beginning to feel that she was actually getting somewhere at last. She must be close to discovering *something*: why else would so many attempts be made to kill, injure or just plain scare her away?

Even more than that, Gil Singleton's very genuine concern for her, as well as his anger at Randy Woodward for putting her in danger in the first place, had been incredibly flattering. More than that, it implied that he wasn't involved at all in the business that had brought her here in the first place, and that was something of a relief to her.

She remembered the way he'd held her earlier that afternoon, the feel of his arms encircling her, pulling her close. She couldn't have escaped, even had she wanted to — and it startled her now to learn that *escape* had been the last thing on her mind.

When there was a soft rap at the door, she sprang up off the bed, thinking that it might be Gil, coming to check on her. She was understandably disappointed, then, when it turned out to be Randall Woodward.

The stocky ranch-hand treated her to a surly look and growled, 'Mind if I come in?'

Without waiting for a reply, he stamped inside.

He looked to be in a foul temper.

Wheeling around, he waited until she closed the door, then said, 'Now, I don't know what tales you've been spreading about me, lady, but they darn near cost me my job.'

'I haven't told *any* tales.'

'Well, let me tell you this. Mr Keyes told me there was a cow'n a calf needed rounding up, just like I told *you*. Where the bull came from, I've got no idea. But when you got proof to the contrary, *that's* when you can start making accusations. Unless you *like* playing me and Gil off against each other, that is.'

She frowned. 'I beg your pardon?'

His sneer was a cold, unpleasant thing. 'Oh, now, don't play the innocent! You know he's as interested in you as I am. But if you think you can play us off against each other, you can think *again*.'

'If I drew the wrong conclusion about you, I'm sorry,' she said coolly. 'But now I think you'd better leave.'

He crossed to the door. 'I'm going, believe me. I said what I wanted to say.'

After he left, Kate sank down on the edge of the bed. Regardless of what she thought of him, Randy had seemed sincere, and she was inclined to believe that he had acted in good faith, that someone *else* had set her up to encounter the bull.

She stretched out on the bed and tried to sleep. She wasn't especially tired, but she wanted to kill time until everyone else went to bed. She had wasted enough of her visit so far. She would waste no more. Tonight she was going to find the evidence she needed once and for all.

*   *   *

Somehow she must have dozed off, because when she opened her eyes again it was a little after two in the morning and the house was as quiet as a tomb.

She rolled silently off the bed, her breathing shallow and nervous, took a small flashlight from her bag and checked that it was working. After the briefest hesitation, she took the gun as well, and stuffed it into the right-side pocket of her body-warmer. Then she slipped from the room.

The hallway outside was in darkness. She waited a moment for her eyes to adjust to the gloom. Somewhere down-stairs, she could just about hear the

86

slow ticking of a grandfather clock in the family room. She snuck along to the head of the stairs, making little or no noise, then descended slowly, being careful to keep her weight on the outside of each step to avoid any unwelcome creaks.

On the ground floor, she paused for a moment, listening to the night. There was hardly any sound now, just that of her own fluttery exhalations.

She ghosted through the house until she reached the door to Glenn Keyes' office.

Even as she reached out and took hold of the door handle, however, there came a sudden stirring of movement behind her.

Before she could turn and cry out, she was caught in a tight grip, one hand snaking around to trap her arms at her sides, the other clamping her mouth shut.

With a barely-audible grunt, her assailant dragged her back into the darkness.

6

The next few seconds were filled with confusion. She struggled to break the hold, but his arms might just as well have been steel bands. There was no give in them at all.

Through the living room she was dragged, on through the kitchen toward the back door. She tried to kick at her assailant's shins, but he deftly side-stepped her every move.

Then his voice rasped in her ear, his mouth so close that she could feel the warmth of his breath.

'*Not a sound.*'

The hand left her mouth just long enough to unlock the door. Then it clamped back over her lower face, she was dragged out into the night, turned around and hoisted unceremoniously over the man's right shoulder.

He moved faster now, as he weaved

through the thick shadows, taking her away from the house, skirting around the cabins and finally depositing her back on her feet in a small clearing on the far side of the lake.

Breathing hard, scared and angry in equal measure, Kate made a grab for the gun in her pocket, but the man now facing her said out of the darkness, 'There's no need for that. We're on the same side — I think.'

The voice froze her.

'*Gil!*' she breathed.

He took off his Stetson. The moonlight showed her his long, slightly sad face, his square jaw and grim mouthline.

'I think it's about time we had words, Miss Kate.'

She brushed herself down, her breathing gradually settling. 'Really? What — '

'Let's not play any more games,' he cut in. 'You're up to something here, and I want to know what it is.'

'I don't know — '

'You're carrying a gun,' he snapped. 'You've made two attempts that I know of to get into Mr Keyes' office, and someone around here has made two attempts to either kill you or scare you off. Why?'

She shook her head. 'You've got it all wrong . . .'

'I don't think so,' he replied. And from his jeans' pocket he produced a long brass cartridge shell. 'You didn't just fall off your horse yesterday. Someone took a pot-shot at you. I went back there this morning, took a look around and found this in the grass.

'And then there was that business today. We don't often confuse bulls with calves, Miss Kate. Someone was out to hurt you or scare you. I thought as much earlier, that's why I followed you out to Bluebird Canyon. So I'm asking you again — *why?*'

The events of the day, coupled with the events of the night, were threatening to leave Kate dizzy. She saw a deadfall log not far away and went over to sit on it. The night was cool, the surrounding trees and the calm surface of the lake silvered by the strong moonlight. Hugging herself, she said 'What did you mean just now? When you said we were both on the same side?'

He followed her over and dropped to his haunches before her. Again, she noticed that he winced ever so slightly, as if in pain. He made nothing of it, though, and a moment later he was back to his usual tough self. 'You go first,' he countered.

Kate took a deep breath. Although she was as sure as she could be that she could trust him, there was still a tiny part of her that urged caution. She was intrigued by the comment he'd made about them being on the same side, though: and much as she hated to admit it, she felt that she could use an ally about now.

'My name *is* Kate Weaver,' she said softly. 'I work for the Cattle Raiser's Association.'

'Oh?'

'As part of the rustling unit.'

'I figured it was something like that,' he said after a moment, and she thought she detected a hint of disappointment in his voice. 'Seeing the gun and all. That's why I decided to keep an eye on you.'

She went on, 'For some time now, you've had quite a problem with cattle rustling in this area.'

'Yup. All over.'

'But Meadow Spring hasn't suffered anywhere near the same number of losses as any of the other ranches, which leads us to believe that the rustlers have been told to go easy on Meadow Spring stock . . . '

' . . . or they're right here, and only taking a fraction of the stock so's not to make it look too obvious,' he finished.

She nodded.

'So you're here to break this rustling ring once and for all, are you?' he asked. She bristled at the sarcasm in his tone.

'I'm here to get evidence,' she

corrected. 'As soon as we can get enough good, hard evidence, we can move, get a warrant to search the place from top to bottom.'

'Well, if you don't mind me saying, you haven't done too well up to now.' He studied her for a long pair of seconds, then asked, 'Are you *really* from the Cattle Raiser's Association?'

She stiffened. 'Of course I am!'

'Well, you sure don't act like any investigator *I've* ever seen before.'

She was about to offer him a scathing reply when she thought better of it. He was right, of course. Oh, she *did* work for the rustling unit, as she'd said. But only in an administrative capacity. This was her first — and probably last — field mission.

To most people, cattle rustling was a thing of the past, something that went on in the 1880s that was now little more than ancient history. But the truth was very different. Rustlers were still active in every state where they raised cattle, and with prices so strong that one trailer-load alone could fetch in tens of thousands of dollars, the risks were well worth taking.

Not that the cattle were rustled solely for meat. The calves of stolen livestock were frequently sold off soon after birth in order to bolster thinning herds elsewhere.

Of course, the penalties were high, too. Rustlers could expect to spend ten years in jail if they were caught. So it was only to be expected that they could and often did play rough.

But though the problem was a serious one, the Cattle Raiser's Association only had limited funds to deal with it. The rustling unit could boast eighteen investigators — the modern day equivalent of the old-time ranch detectives. But the investigators in Kate's unit alone were stretched thin over Colorado, Wyoming, Kansas, New Mexico and Texas. They simply did not have the man-power to deal with the problem.

And the problem in and around the

Meadow Spring area had been growing steadily worse for some time when Kate had suggested that she go to Meadow Spring Ranch, posing as a tourist, and try to confirm or refute the suspicions of the unit. With little choice in the matter, and with his own superiors running out of patience and demanding results, her beleaguered boss had reluctantly agreed.

Not that she had done much of a job so far, she had to confess.

Doug had played his part in it too, of course. And as she remembered him again, her face clouded. The way things had ended between them had left her hurt, confused and with a pretty low opinion of herself. She realized now that she had put herself forward for this assignment to rebuild her shattered confidence.

'Anyway,' she said, picking up the conversation, 'that's where I fit into this business. Now it's your turn.'

He didn't speak at once. In fact, even in the poor light, she could see just how ill-at-ease he was. And she could understand his discomfort. He probably hated to speak ill of anyone, least of all the people who paid his wages.

'I've worked at Meadow Spring just about all my life, just like my pa and grandpa before me,' he explained. 'Used to be a *good* place to work, too, but times change. The original owners got old, didn't have no kin to leave the place to, so they sold it on to the Keyes'.'

'And that's when things changed?'

'I guess. They wanted to keep the place as a working ranch, but they also had this idea to open it up to vacationers, so they built the cabins, stocked the lake with trout, started advertising. My thinking is that they spent a sight more money on the place than they meant to, that though it was popular enough as a dude ranch, it's been nowhere near as popular as all their business projections suggested, and that they ran into money troubles.'

'So they turned to cattle rustling?' she prodded.

Again he shook his head. 'I don't know. They're good people. I can't see them master-minding this kind of operation. But I think I can give you that proof you've been looking for.'

She stiffened. *'What?'*

'I reached pretty much the same conclusion as your people at the Cattle Raiser's Association. Just about every cattle spread in these parts has been hit worse than we have. So I started looking around for some evidence of my own. I found it that-a-way.'

Gesturing with one hand, he went on, 'Away to the southeast, the land breaks up into a maze of canyons, cut-backs and dry washes. They twist and turn back on themselves until you can hardly remember which way is up any more.

'Well, one day I chanced upon some cattle tracks heading that way and decided to see where they took me. They petered out after a while, but I kept going back and looking around. Eventually I happened across a cabin, a couple of outbuildings and a few holding pens, tucked away where no one else would ever suspect 'em. I reckon that's where they take the rustled cattle. It's a kind of halfway house, if you like, where they can change their brands and then ship 'em out again under cover of darkness.'

He glanced off across the lake, looking wretched. 'I've been trying to figure out what to do about it for a while now. As much as anything else, I don't know who else is involved, who I can trust. Don't even know for sure that they're using the halfway house to rustle cattle, though I'm pretty certain. I guess you coming along has finally taken the matter out of my hands.'

He pushed back to his feet and put his hat back on. 'Well,' he finished, 'you've got your evidence. Get out of here at first light and tell your bosses they could do worse than check that place out.'

She got to her feet too, came closer to look up at him. 'I need more than just your word,' she said. 'I need evidence, to see this place for myself, take some pictures.'

'My word not good enough?' he bit back.

'Well that figures. Sometimes you want to believe, even when you know you shouldn't.'

She frowned. 'What's that supposed to mean?'

'Aw, nothing.'

'Well, I need to see this halfway house for myself. Will you take me there?'

'Might be dangerous.'

'I'll risk it if you will.'

'I'll do it, if it helps put them rustlers behind bars. But I won't enjoy it. Whether they're in this rustling business or not, Mr and Mrs Keyes, they've been decent to me.'

Again she felt some of the conflict inside him, the need to do the right thing, the reluctance to hurt the people involved any more than he had to.

'When can we go?' she asked gently.

He gave the question a moment's thought. 'Randy's taking some of the guests on a hike up to Medwell tomorrow. You probably heard about it.'

She had. It was an eighteen-mile round trip with an overnight stay in the high country, taking in the local ghost town, mine workings and prehistoric Indian site Blanche had mentioned during their first conversation.

'Tell him you want to go along. Early afternoon, tell him you're not feeling so good, that you'll head back to the ranch and rest up.'

'What about you?'

'I'll find some excuse to go missing and trail you. Soon as I see you split from the group, I'll come get you and take you to the halfway house. You do what you have to do, and then we get out of there, pronto, right? There's a lot of money to be made from this game, and we already know how rough they can get.'

She nodded, suddenly chilled. As she looked up into his face, which was now draped in shadow, she remembered what had happened between them that afternoon. After a moment she said, 'Gil . . .'

'Yes, Miss Kate?'

'I *can* trust you, can't I? About this?'

'Sure,' he said, adding, 'About *this*.'

She eyed him carefully. 'Meaning . . . ?'

'Meaning I'm on your side, just like I said. But what I did earlier — what we did earlier, I mean — that was nothing. Just a spur of the moment thing. I shouldn't have done it, and I've regretted it ever since.'

Her voice was suddenly small. 'Oh.'

He made a loose, embarrassed gesture. 'I guess I just got caught up in the moment . . .'

'Me too,' she agreed quickly. *Too* quickly.

'Well, we'd best be getting back to the ranch,' he said, his manner suddenly, hurtfully formal. 'One way or another, tomorrow's going to be a busy day.'

Waking early the following morning after a near-sleepless night, Kate showered and dressed more by habit than anything else, her thoughts elsewhere.

Her unexpected encounter with Gil had given her a lot to think about — and not just about the rustling ring. She wanted to feel relieved that the kiss they'd shared had, as he'd said, been nothing more than a spur of the moment thing, something of no great consequence. After all, it was too soon, if ever, to consider falling in love again. It was too painful when things went wrong, as she knew only too well.

So yes, she should feel relief.

And yet she felt more disappointment than anything else, and she hated herself for it. After all, hadn't she learned *anything* from what had happened with Doug?

To make matters worse, she felt embarrassment, too. For a while there she'd believed that Gil had been as attracted to her as she was to him. And yet now she understood that his only interest in her had been based on suspicion, because he'd seen the gun and wondered if she was something more than the tourist she was pretending to be.

The weather had taken a turn for the worse. An unseasonably cool wind had blown in from the north and brought with it an ominous gathering of dark rain-clouds. Glancing out of her window, she wondered whether or not the hike would be postponed. She hoped not. It was the perfect excuse for her to get away from the ranch without arousing too much suspicion, and see this mysterious halfway house for herself. If she could get enough photographic evidence, her mission would be accomplished.

Then, appearing to take Glenn Keyes' advice, she could leave early, hand the evidence over to her boss, and within twenty-four hours Meadow

Spring Ranch would be swarming with county police officers, working in collaboration with the Cattle Raiser's Association.

And Gil Singleton's way of life, she suddenly realized, would be finished for good. The ranch upon which his father and grandfather had both worked before him would be closed down, broken up, sold off, and even if it continued as a ranch under different ownership, it would never be the same for him.

He must have known that. Perhaps that was why he'd hesitated for so long before deciding to act upon his suspicions. And yet the instinctive disgust every genuine cowboy felt for rustlers had eventually won out. Even though it might spell the end of his livelihood, he had still elected to do the right thing.

She was relieved to discover that the hike was still on. Glenn Keyes seemed surprised that she wanted to go along, especially at such short notice, but said he didn't guess it presented much of a problem.

'Better just make sure it's all right with Randy,' he concluded.

She found Woodward checking a string of saddled horses in the barn. His expression hardened noticeably when he saw her coming.

'Help you?' he asked shortly.

Kate had been thinking about something else Gil Singleton had said the previous night — that he wasn't sure whom he could trust. Now, as she looked up at the stocky cowhand, she had the same feeling. Was Randy Woodward part of the rustling ring? She wouldn't be altogether surprised.

'I'd like to go on the hike,' she replied 'if it's not too late. Mr Keyes said it would be okay.'

He shrugged. 'Well, he's the boss,' was his terse reply. 'I'll go saddle you a horse and arrange some supplies for the overnight stop. We leave in forty minutes.'

True to his word, Randy led his little

group out within the hour. About six of the guests had signed on to make the round-trip, including the newlyweds and Dan and Joe.

The procession set out in high spirits, despite the inclement weather. Kate, riding at the rear, took one quick glance back as the ranch fell behind them, but saw no sign of Gil.

Randy set an easy pace as he led his group across flat prairie toward the distant, smoothly rounded contours of a rising series of timbered hills. Dropping back for a while, he asked if anyone would care to hazard a guess how far away the hills were.

'Six miles,' Dan Collins said at once.

'Less than that,' decided his friend. 'I can almost count the trees.' He hesitated for a moment, then said, 'Three miles.'

'Actually, they're about twelve miles away,' Randy replied.

'You're kidding!'

'No, sir. The secret's in the air. It's so clear at this elevation that it makes everything look closer than it really is.' He threw Kate a cool grin. 'You'll be saddle-sore by the time we reach them, I promise you.'

The morning wore on. Randy pointed out mountain mahogany shrubs and made them ride past something called skunk bush, which gave off a foul odour. There was hawkweed and sow-thistle, bind-weed and wild geraniums, and under any other circumstances Kate would have been fascinated. But right now her mind was on other things.

They followed a pleasant stream for several miles, and here they saw a bighorn ram drinking beyond a stand of small tamarisk trees. The land was vast, the trail winding but fortunately, very clearly defined. More than once Kate searched their surroundings for any sign of Gil, but if he was out there, as he'd promised to be, then he was very well concealed.

At noon Randy called a halt, built a small fire and brewed coffee for everyone. Though tired by the long ride, the mood of the hikers was still high, and Randy received a number of well-earned compliments for the fine job he'd performed so far.

Distracted though she'd been, Kate had to concede that he had made the ride a real pleasure. His knowledge of the land and its secrets seemed to be endless. But now she felt she must leave the group and hope to be met by Gil.

Rubbing her forehead for effect, she sought Randy out and told him that she wasn't feeling too good. The big cowhand shook his head and sucked in a breath. 'What's the problem?' he asked impatiently.

She shrugged. 'Headache. Nausea. I didn't sleep too well last night.'

'It doesn't sound too bad.'

'It isn't. But I'm afraid that riding up into the foothills isn't going to make it any better.'

'Well, that's too bad. We got a schedule to keep, so we can't stick around until you feel better. And before you ask, we're not about to turn back.'

'I don't expect you to,' she replied. 'I'll just rest here for a while, if that's okay. If I feel better I'll catch you up. If not, I'll go back to the ranch.'

He gave her an emphatic shake of the head. 'Oh, no. I'm not having you wandering around out here all by yourself. You can go back, sure. The trail's easy enough to follow. But you're not going on and risk getting lost.'

She nodded. 'All right. I'll go back. I'm sorry . . .'

He waved her apology away. 'Just get yourself back to the ranch,' he growled irritably.

Word quickly spread to the other hikers, who showed considerably more concern for her welfare than Randy had. Joe Fulford even offered to accompany her, just to make sure she got back to Meadow Spring in one piece.

Kate hated having to pretend, especially when the concern being expressed was so genuine, but she couldn't turn back now.

'I'll be fine,' she assured them. 'All I need is an aspirin and some sleep.'

By this time, Randy had tightened his saddle strap, and was urging the others to do likewise. 'You heard her, folks,' he called. 'She'll be okay. Now see to your horses. We're moving out!'

Kate watched them clean up after themselves and then remount. They moved out at a comfortable trot, some of them hipping around to wave to her before they vanished beyond the next belt of trees.

The wind picked up and ruffled the grass and the surface of the nearby stream with its cold hand. Its low, mournful keening made her feel uneasy, as did the heavy, purple clouds pressing down from above.

Then a voice behind her said, 'That was quite a performance. Even *I* believed you were sickening for something.'

She spun around to find Gil standing in some brush thirty feet away, holding the reins of his horse loosely in his left hand. He wore a brown box jacket buttoned to the throat, and had pulled his Stetson low over his short, sandy hair against the persistent tug of the wind. In that moment he looked exactly like an old-time cowboy who had somehow stepped out of the past, and her heart quickened at the sight of him.

'It wasn't something I enjoyed,' she replied as he led his horse closer. 'I'm just not cut out for deception.'

He raised one eyebrow. 'Then you're a very rare woman indeed,' he decided. 'Are you ready to ride?'

'Yes.'

'And have you got your gun?'

'Yes.'

'Good.' And here his eyes grew bleak. 'Because if this thing goes wrong, we might just need it.'

7

The rain came about an hour later. It started as a fine drizzle and gradually increased until the horses were splashing awkwardly through muddy puddles and visibility had dropped by more than half. In the distance lightning turned the overcast sky a cool blue before plunging it back to its deeper purple, and thunder growled a constant, ominous warning.

Earlier, Gil had drawn rein and studied the terrain ahead as best he could. Kate reined to a halt beside him, her horse side-stepping nervously. Gil reached over with one hand and took hold of the bridle, muttering nonsense words to calm her mount and his own. At length he said, 'We're in for a hard rain, looks like. We'd better fort up somewheres.'

They'd made good progress since

Kate had left the other hikers, though how Gil knew where he was going remained a constant source of amazement to her.

He had led her into a bewildering series of canyons, riding largely in silence. But that was fine with Kate. She hadn't felt much like talking herself. Soon the trail began to curve like a snake as it wound between sheer rock walls, and the only sound was the clatter and echo of their horse's hooves as they pushed ever deeper into the broken country.

Alone with her thoughts, it came to Kate that this land was completely at odds with the lush prairie they had just left behind them. But of course there was life here too, from the hackberry trees that rose up from a thin streambed to the brightly-coloured lizard she saw skittering across cracked rocks and on to the muledeer bucks she spotted grazing on the sparse grass. The canyon walls themselves were layered, as if one sheet of rock had been set upon another, and another, and so on, until they lifted toward the sky and threw the trail which passed between them into almost permanent shade.

She realised also that it must have taken considerable persistence before Gil finally discovered the halfway house, and that the rustlers could have wished for no more isolated spot to conduct their criminal business.

But all the while the storm clouds kept building, adding to her growing sense of unease. Over time the wind picked up, and it was a cold one that made her shiver and zip her jacket to the chin.

And then, at last, had come the rain.

'Where can we shelter?' she asked, having to raise her voice to be heard above the downpour, and its constant accompaniment of low, rumbling thunder.

To her relief, he gestured with his left hand. 'There's a cave up ahead. Nothing fancy, I'm afraid, but it'll keep us dry.'

She nodded, eyes narrowed at the deluge. 'Lead on.'

He took the reins from her hands and then moved out, leading her across a slope covered in loose shale. She held onto the saddle horn for safety. The rain was coming down harder now, hammering at her baseball cap and shoulders, plastering the horse's mane to its long, sleek neck. All at once the noise was deafening, what little light there was dimmed to an eerie gloom.

She had no idea how long they forged on through the storm. It seemed like an hour, but was probably no more than fifteen minutes. At last he drew to a halt and dismounted, gesturing for her to do the same. Then he began to lead the horses up over a steep, uneven path that rose toward a long, rocky shelf, and half-blinded now by the needling rain, she stumbled after him.

The wind had strengthened and threatened to pluck her from the path. But then they reached the shelf above and she saw Gil lead the horses toward a cleft in the canyon wall.

The fissure opened out into a fairly spacious cave with a low, shadowy ceiling and a sandy floor. As she paused in the opening and peeled her cap from her bedraggled hair, Gil led the horses down to the far end.

'I'll get a fire going in a while, and then we can dry off,' he said over one shoulder.

While she regained her breath, and the storm finally began to hit the canyon lands with its full force, he gathered what little dead wood had been deposited across the cave floor during past floods and built a fire. Its restless amber light added some cheer to their surroundings and helped chase away the lingering chill.

'Why don't you fix us some coffee?' he suggested as he busied himself off-saddling the horses and drying them down.

She found a small coffee pot and beans in one of his saddlebags, filled the pot with water from her canteen and then set the pot on the fire to boil. It was strange, sharing this crude sanctuary with him. It seemed so intimate that it didn't feel *right*, somehow. And yet, in another way, it seemed very, *very* right indeed.

'Better change out of those wet clothes,' he went on without turning around. 'You did *bring* a change, didn't you?'

'Well, yes, but — '

'You'd better change, then, unless you want to catch pneumonia,' he told her briskly.

Still she hesitated, until he finally shook his head. 'Go on,' he urged. 'I promise not to peek.'

He was right, of course. She was soaked to the skin. And this was hardly the time for modesty. Quickly she stripped and slipped into the dry jeans and sweater she took from her own saddlebags, draping the wet clothes over her upturned saddle so that they could dry by the fire.

When he was finished with the

horses, Gil also changed. Kate kept her eyes on the floor of the cave, listening to the soft sounds he made stripping. But the temptation to look up was insistent in her, and would not be denied.

Finally she gave in to it and chanced a look at him. He had his back to her. The firelight played over his broad shoulders and muscular arms, down along the dip of his spine, tracing every line and contour of his bronzed skin.

She was startled to find that her mouth had gone dry, that in those few seconds she had forgotten to keep breathing. Then it occurred to her that maybe, just maybe, he had given in to temptation and stolen a look at *her*, as well, and she blushed furiously and was just about to look away when he turned, buttoning his jeans, and she saw his chest.

She couldn't hide her look of surprise, for there was a barely-visible patchwork of pale white scars along his left side, extending from his hip to his pectoral.

He stared at her, waiting for her to speak. All she could manage was, 'I ... I'm sorry. I didn't mean to stare.'

He pulled on a collarless blue shirt and tucked it into his waistband. 'That coffee ready yet?' he asked, as if he hadn't just caught her gawking at him. 'I could sure use some.'

'Ah, yes. Here.'

She poured coffee into two enamel cups and he came to settle on the far side of the fire from her, wincing almost imperceptibly as he did so.

She remembered the other times she'd seen him show pain or discomfort, immediately linked them to the scars and felt her curiosity building all over again.

'Are you all right?' she asked.

'Yup.'

'It's just that — '

'I'm fine,' he cut in, silencing her. 'It's this wet weather. I've got an old injury and it plays up sometimes.'

'What happened?' she asked.

'None of your business,' he replied shortly.

She leaned back as if slapped. 'I'm sorry,' she said again.

Outside, the rain continued to slam earthwards, the thunder to growl and cause the cool air to tremble. Lightning burst across the sky, lighting the cave entrance before throwing it back into darkness. Kate shivered.

He said, 'No. *I'm* sorry.'

'Forget it.'

'No,' he said again. 'I had no call to use that tone on you. You asked a perfectly reasonable question.'

He blew steam off his coffee, sipped it. Then he took a small silver flask from his saddlebags and tipped some of its contents into his cup to fortify the brew. 'Here,' he said. 'It's brandy. It'll help chase the chills away.'

Although she tried to refuse, he added a shot to her coffee anyway.

'I used to compete in rodeos,' he said. 'They hold a state-wide show every summer, and I used to represent

Meadow Spring. I used to barrel race and tie-down rope, and wrestle steers — you know, grab 'em by the horns and wrestle 'em to the ground. I was pretty good at it, too. But I guess what you'd call my speciality was bull riding.'

'Bull riding?'

'Yes'm. You ride a bull the way you'd ride a horse, 'cept you don't have a saddle, and a bull is a whole lot meaner than a horse could ever be. The idea is to stay astride for at least eight seconds.

'Well, about two years ago I entered one such event, managed ten seconds and could've gone a little longer, except that the bull slipped and fell. Critter landed right on top of me.'

Kate murmured, 'My God . . . '

He nodded. 'Yes'm. Sixteen hundred pounds of prime beef on the hoof. By rights they should've scooped me off the ground like so much paste, and for sure I was more dead than alive when they finally got me outta there . . . ' His eyes took on a far away look, then suddenly sharpened again. 'But I was lucky, had some good doctors and I pulled through. That satisfy you?'

She studied him for a long moment before saying, 'Not really.'

Surprise showed briefly in his expression. 'Why not?'

Emboldened by the brandy, she said, 'Because I don't think you're telling me the whole story. There's something else, isn't there?'

He drained his mug, clearly uncomfortable. '*Is* there? Strikes me, you seem to know more about it than I do.'

'You see?' she countered. 'If there wasn't anything else, you wouldn't be so defensive. But don't worry, it's personal, I can see that. And the last thing I want to do is pry.'

He eyed her sidelong, his familiar scowl back in place. 'I'm glad to hear it.' He glanced toward the cave entrance. 'I got a feeling we're going to be stuck here for the night. You hungry?'

'Yes.'

'Then we'll rustle up something to

eat, bed down early and get a fresh start in the morning.'

'That sounds fine,' she agreed stiffly.

Between them they cobbled together a rough-and-ready supper of vacuum-packed hot dogs, beans and cut sweet potatoes. It was very basic fare, but Kate couldn't tell when she last enjoyed a meal so much.

Partway through, Gil surprised her by saying, 'You were right, by the way. There *was* more to it than I let on.'

She glanced up from her plate. 'It's okay. I really *didn't* mean to pry.'

But the brandy had loosened his tongue. 'It was a girl,' he went on, as if he hadn't heard her. 'Lynne. I guess I thought she'd done hung the moon, and flattered myself to think she felt the same way about me. 'Fact, I was figuring to propose to her when I had the accident.'

'And that changed everything?' Kate asked softly.

'Kind of. Just after it happened, and I was taken to the hospital, she looked down at me and told me I'd be okay, that she'd be right there when I came out of surgery. I guess she really figured I was going to die, just like everyone else did, and wanted me to feel a sight easier about it.

'Anyway, I told her I loved her. Leastways, I *tried* to. I was pretty much out of it at the time, but I remembered what she told *me*. She said she loved me. That no matter how long it took, she'd wait for me, be there when I came back.

'Then I went into the operating room and didn't know much else about it for the next three weeks. I guess I came about as close to dying then as I was ever likely to. But when I finally regained consciousness . . . '

His voice trailed off.

'Lynne was gone?' she guessed.

'Yup. Lynne was gone. Turned out that the girl who'd said she'd wait for me actually lasted about a week. Then one of the interns caught her eye and she decided it was better to have a whole boyfriend than the crippled one she figured she'd end up with — *if* I lived at all, that is.'

'But you *did* live, and you're as good as you were before.'

'Pretty much,' he allowed. 'It took a while, but I got there in the end. Wouldn't allow myself not to. I guess I thought I might win her back.'

'Even though she deserted you?'

'Like I say, I was crazy about her, and you know what they say about love being blind.' His brief smile was humourless. 'I'd bought a little place down around Cameron Pass, figured to raise horses there and I wanted her to come and live the dream with me. But by then she didn't want to know. She was a city girl, didn't want to trade that for the simple life.'

'Do you still have your place?'

'Ah, sure. Don't ever go down there, though. Not much point now.'

Before she could stop herself she said, 'I never had you down as the kind of man who'd feel sorry for himself.'

His jaw clenched tight. 'I'm not.'

'You *weren't*,' she allowed. 'You could've given up the day you regained consciousness in that hospital bed, but you didn't. You fought your way back to health instead.'

He shrugged. 'If you want the truth of it, sometimes I wondered why I bothered. I'm just old-fashioned enough to believe that a man needs a woman, that he should share his life and his dreams with someone he can love and trust, and who loves and trusts *him*. Guess that sounds kind of naïve, doesn't it?' He waved one hand dismissively. 'Ah, forget it.'

She set her plate aside, an odd sense of excitement suddenly building within her. 'It left you feeling as if you could never trust a woman again, didn't it?' she said gently.

Grudgingly he replied, 'I haven't met a woman yet who'd make me change my mind.'

'Well, I've got news for you, Gil,' she went on. 'You don't have the monopoly on broken hearts, you know.'

He watched her sombrely. 'You too, huh?' he asked softly.

She nodded.

And somehow all the things she'd kept bottled up inside her suddenly came boiling to the surface, the words coming from her in a rush, a purging, cleansing rush.

* * *

She'd met Doug Shannon soon after going to work for the Cattle Raiser's Association, about six or seven months earlier. He had been in public relations, a charismatic, smooth-talker with black hair, green eyes and a winning smile, maybe five or six years older than her.

They'd gotten along well on the few occasions that her work brought her into contact with him, and Kate had been both surprised and delighted when he'd finally asked her out.

They went for a meal, a movie and drinks afterward, and in all respects he was the perfect gentleman. Kate, her own experience with men fairly limited, had quickly fallen in love with him.

There was just one problem, however — Susan.

She called and texted him constantly, and always much to his embarrassment. Apparently, she had been his last girlfriend. They'd split up two years earlier, but the split had been amicable.

Kate was prepared to accept that. After all, it had said a lot for Doug that there were no hard feelings between them. What she found difficult were his constant references to her. Susan hated Italian food. Green was Susan's favourite colour. Susan had come from a large family. Susan had the cutest laugh.

One night, Kate told Doug that she really didn't need to keep hearing about Susan. The revelation — though it should hardly have come as such — silenced him for awhile. A few moments later he said, 'I'm not quite sure what you mean.'

Awkwardly, for it wasn't anything she enjoyed saying, she told him, 'I think you're still in love with her, Doug.'

'That's crazy!'

'And I don't think there can be any future for us until you move on.'

His mouth had dropped open. 'Are you saying you want to break up with me?'

'No. I'm just saying that if you want us to be a couple, then that's what we have to be. Two people, not *three*.'

He shook his head. 'You're wrong,' he said softly. 'Susan's the past, you're the present. You're the *future*.'

And he'd closed one hand over hers.

That should have been an end to it, of course. But it wasn't. A few nights later, Doug arrived at Kate's apartment. They'd planned to take in a show. But just as Kate was fetching her jacket, his cell phone rang. It was Susan.

They spoke together for the next hour, and every time Kate pointed meaningfully at her watch, Doug's only response was a helpless shrug and a shake of the head.

Long before the conversation came to a close, she went into her bedroom and changed out of her dress and into jeans and a sweatshirt. There was no way they'd make it to the theatre now.

Of course, Doug was properly contrite afterwards. 'I'm sorry, honey, I really am. But I just couldn't get rid of her.'

Curiously, Kate hadn't felt jealous, only annoyed. 'Why don't you just face it, Doug? You can't let her go, can you? Any more than *she* can let *you* go.'

Stubbornly he shook his head. 'She's just someone I used to know, that's all. I don't *love* her, not any more.' And suddenly he fell quiet, stared her fully in the face. 'It's *you* I love,' he said softly.

It was the first time any man had told her that, and he said it with such conviction that she had no reason to doubt him.

'Oh, Doug . . . '

He reached for her and closed his

arms around her and kissed her with a passion she'd never known before, and which left her breathless.

'Have you ever heard of the Call of the Wild?' he asked when they finally broke apart.

'No. What is it?'

'It's a retreat up in the hills. We'll rent a log cabin. We can ski, hike, check out the snow-mobiles or simply shop,' he said. 'They have hot springs, too, so we can even skinny-dip, if we like! And in the evenings we can settle down together and let the rest of the world take care of itself.' He stared into her eyes, fired up by the prospect. 'What do you say?'

A week later he drove them up to the cabin park, still excited by the long weekend ahead of them. And his excitement was infectious. Kate felt that they had finally turned a corner in their relationship — that everything was going to be okay from now on.

The cabins were set apart from each other in a valley surrounded by blue-grey peaks. Their cabin was a rustic affair nestled amid low trees. It contained everything they would need and more besides. The master bedroom boasted a queen-sized bed. The living room had a phone and satellite TV. The refrigerator was fully-stocked — even to three bottles of Krug Grand Cuvée Doug had ordered especially for the occasion.

Kate didn't believe she'd ever felt happier than she did in that moment.

'We've even got our own private hot tub,' he said, sliding back one of the patio doors in the bedroom.

She watched him inspect the tub, an uneasy thought coming to mind.

'Have you been here before?' she asked, her tone deceptively casual.

He nodded. 'Yeah. Me and Susan — '

He fell silent.

Disbelief reduced Kate's voice to a whisper. 'You brought me to the same cabin you shared with Susan . . . ?'

Before he could reply, his cell phone bleeped: a text had just come in. He checked the screen, then put the phone back in his pocket.

'Who was that?' she asked.

His silence confirmed her suspicion.

'Please, Kate. Just forget what I said. It's *you* I want to be with. *You're* the one I love.'

'Don't tell me,' she replied. 'Tell *Susan.*'

He had ample opportunity. Susan texted him every twenty minutes or so for the rest of the day.

Things finally came to a head about seven o'clock that night. The texts had stopped coming a couple of hours earlier, and Kate had somehow convinced herself that Susan had finally gotten the message.

But just as Kate started dinner, there was a knock at the cabin door. She and Doug exchanged a look. He looked sick.

'Answer it,' she said.

'I — '

'She's not going to go away,' Kate told him.

Reluctantly Doug answered the door, and as it swung back, Kate got her first look at the woman who had haunted their relationship for so long.

'We need to talk,' said the newcomer, brushing past him, uninvited, into the cabin. But she wasn't at all what Kate had been expecting.

Susan was of average height and a little overweight. She wore her black hair to shoulder length, with a left-side part. She was dressed in a neat two-piece suit, skirt and jacket, in pale cream. Her blue blouse was open at the neck, at which she wore a string of pearls. For want of a better word, she simply looked . . . *ordinary*.

Seeing Kate, she came to a halt and raised one eyebrow. '*You*,' she said in a low, controlled voice, 'must be his latest conquest.'

'And you're Susan,' returned Kate, standing her ground.

The other woman showed surprise. 'You've heard of me, then?'

'I've heard *all* about you.'

'Then you'll know why I'm here.'

'I think so.'

'Susan . . . ' murmured Doug, speaking for the first time. He sounded nervous, anxious to avoid the confrontation he knew was coming.

Ignoring him, still addressing Kate, Susan said, 'What is it that you know, then? Or *think* you know?'

Drawing a breath, Kate said, 'You're going to tell me you want Doug back, aren't you?'

'Something like that.'

'Well, I'm going to tell *you* something,' Kate went on. 'I don't think you want Doug as much as you *say* you do. I think you've only developed this sudden interest in him all over again because he's moved on and finally left you behind, and you don't like that.'

'Is *that* what you believe?'

'Are you going to deny it?'

Susan pursed her lips. 'You poor, foolish girl,' she said.

Again Doug muttered, 'Susan . . . '

But, still ignoring him, Susan said, 'I

want him back, it's true. But only because his children idolise him, and I feel that their father should be there for them.'

'Chil — !'

The revelation struck Kate like a blow. She actually rocked back on her heels, frowned, shook her head as if she might somehow rearrange everything so that it actually made sense.

Seeing her reaction, Susan's expression suddenly, surprisingly, softened. 'What exactly did he tell you?' she asked.

Her mind still elsewhere, Kate said vaguely, 'That you and he used to date. That he broke up with you, but you kept pestering him.'

Susan's laugh was short and grim. 'Well, I'm sorry to shatter your illusions,' she said, 'but the truth is very different. We're married. We've been married for nine years, and we have two children, a boy aged seven and a girl who's three. As to the rest of it, there's some truth to it. He *did* walk out on

136

me, on *us*, after making a long and frankly pathetic speech about how he'd married too young and felt trapped by circumstances and wanted to be a free agent again. And I *have* pestered him, but only to try and get him to see sense, if only for the sake of our children.'

Kate shook her head again. It was almost too much to take in all at once. 'W . . . well, if it's any consolation, he talks about you all the time. And now I think I see why. He still loves you.'

Her lipped curled. 'That's too bad. Because whatever feeling I had for *him* — and I *did* love him once, I loved him dearly — whatever there was is gone. All I feel for him now is a kind of pity, and revulsion. But that's my concern. For all his weaknesses, and he has many of them, his children adore him. That's why I tolerate his behaviour. For them.'

Suddenly Kate's attention focused sharply on the other woman.

'Tolerate his behaviour . . . ?'

The flesh between Susan's brows pinched in a frown. 'You really don't *get* it, do you?' she said, not unkindly. 'You're not the first, and you won't be the last. You're just one in a long line of silly, impressionable girls whose main function is simply to make him feel good, and young, and attractive, again. All the things I, apparently, am no longer *able* to do.'

Stunned now, Kate could only look from Susan to Doug, wanting him so desperately to shake his head, deny everything with a vehement, 'Don't listen to her, Kate! She's making it all up to try to drive a wedge between us!'

But Doug wouldn't even meet her gaze, and it was in that moment that she realised the truth: that he had lied to her, toyed with her, that he had turned his back on his own children in order to satisfy his own many vanities, and broken *their* trust and hers.

That he had broken *her*, too.

8

Kate opened her eyes. She had slept heavily, and woke now without properly knowing where she was.

Then she looked around her, saw to her surprise that she was in a cave, its uneven walls pale grey now in the watery early-morning sunlight that filled the entrance.

A *cave?* What on earth was she doing in a —

Before she could finish the thought, one of two horses quartered at the back of the cave whinnied a greeting. Startled by the unaccustomed sound, she turned her head toward it, and realised —

'*Oh!*'

She realised she had been sleeping in the arms of a strange man, snugged tight to his body for warmth against the lingering chill of night!

Instinctively she pulled away from him, the movement causing him to groan and stir. He turned his face towards her, and she realised that he looked familiar. A new memory entered her mind — a flask of brandy that she and this man had drunk between them — and with that she realised she was hung over and remembering everything.

As Gil opened his eyes and saw her propped on one elbow, watching him, he too registered a mixture of surprise and agitation. 'Uh, good morning, Miss Kate,' he said, rolling out from under the blanket and getting to his feet. He was fully dressed, as was she, his clothes now a little crumpled. 'You sleep all right?'

'Yes. A little *too* well, I think.'

'That'll be the brandy. I shouldn't have let you drink so much, but it was cold, and I thought it would put a little life back into you.'

'Please, don't give it another thought.'

He went off to see to their horses,

leaving her to rekindle the small camp fire and boil coffee.

As she worked, her thoughts returned to the previous evening. The brandy had loosened her tongue, made her tell him all about Doug. She had never spoken about that time to anyone. Even afterwards, she had kept everything bottled up inside.

But now she realised that it had been good to get it all out, to share it with another person and, in so doing, to get some perspective on it.

Oh, it had been upsetting. Of course it had. She'd hardly been able to finish her story before the tears came, because she'd been so foolish. But even as the sobs finally shook her body, even as the emotion she had fought so hard and so long to suppress came boiling out of her, Gil was there, gathering her into his embrace, pushing his face into her hair, telling her that everything was okay now, everything was fine . . .

And even as she let all that pain out,

she knew that he was right. She had made a mistake, blaming herself for being so gullible, for allowing a man like Doug to make her feel so special when all along he had simply been using her to make himself feel young and attractive again. After her encounter with Susan, she had fled that cabin at Call of the Wild and blamed herself for everything.

Now, though . . . now she saw that she had been the *victim*, not the perpetrator. It was *Doug* who had been at fault. She had done nothing, save trust a man who had turned out to be anything *but* trustworthy. And somewhere along the line, she had convinced herself that all men were as bad or duplicitous as he.

As she had sobbed into Gil's shoulder and felt his arms tighten around her, giving comfort, she realised that she had been mistaken about *that*, too. Not all men were the same.

Some time later, exhausted by the outpouring of emotion, she had slept in his arms, and he had held her and kept her safe and made no move to exploit the position in which they had found themselves.

They breakfasted on campfire beans and bannock, a doughy kind of bread that was cooked on skewers over the fire. They ate largely in silence. Perhaps Gil was ashamed that he had opened up to her the previous evening. Or maybe he was embarrassed that she had chosen to entrust him with her own demons.

In the circumstances, the only safe topic seemed to be the one that had brought them here in the first place — the halfway house which Gil suspected was being used as the rustlers' base of operations.

'What kind of evidence are you looking for, anyway?' he asked as they started to pack their things away.

She considered. 'Anything that proves that the place is being used to hold cattle, change brands, ship animals out to other places,' she said after a while.

'Tyre tracks, running irons, that kind of thing?'

'Exactly.'

'Means we're gonna have to get in real close, then,' he decided. 'And that could be risky. Near as I can tell, there's four fellers who stay there regularly. I don't know 'em, but they seem pretty set up in that cabin.' He thought some more. 'We'll make our move after dark, just to be on the safe side.'

Kate felt a shiver run through her. 'Gil,' she said suddenly.

'Miss Kate?'

She gave a self-conscious little shrug. 'Thank you. For *this*, I mean. You're putting yourself at risk to help me.'

'I'm doing what I can to bring this rustling business to an end,' he corrected.

'Either way, you've bought into a potentially dangerous game. I just wanted you to know that I appreciate it.'

'Well, if it comes to that, you're putting your*self* at risk to do the same

144

thing. That takes guts.'

She smiled at him. 'I'm in good company, then.'

They pulled out thirty minutes later.

★ ★ ★

The morning was warm and bright, with not even the wispiest cloud to remind them of the previous day's storm. The broken country stretched on ahead and Gil continued to forge straight into it, with Kate riding determinedly beside him.

The winding arroyos, canyons and cut-backs had a weird, eerie silence to them that played on Kate's nerves, but she fought hard to keep her fears in check. Once they came to an arch of rock that spanned the width of the pass. It was a breathtaking natural phenomenon, and passing beneath it was a little like passing through the entrance to a great cathedral.

Gil called a halt around noon and they boiled coffee. Each wondered what they would find waiting for them at journey's end. After a short break they pushed on.

Some time around late afternoon, he raised one hand to stop them again. 'We're close now,' he said softly. 'Best we leave the horses here and go the rest of the way on foot.'

She nodded, and together they dismounted and tied their horses in a small clearing at the centre of a stand of junipers, then began to pick their way up across a shelving incline until they reached its rim, which was littered with boulders of every shape and size.

'Down,' he hissed when they were only yards from the rim, and following his example, she dropped to her stomach and slithered the rest of the way.

'There,' he whispered.

She caught her breath. Set out below them, in what appeared to be a large box canyon, lay a modest scattering of plank-built dwellings, all situated around a dusty front yard. Running her aqua-blue eyes from one to the next, Kate identified a cabin, a dilapidated bunk-house, a storage shed, a barn and two corrals, one larger than the other and joined to its companion by a squeeze chute.

'It looks as if it's been around for a while,' she noted in an undertone.

He nodded. 'About a hundred years or so is my guess. Probably started out as a line camp, then fell into disrepair when there was no more need for it. Then someone rediscovered it and decided to put it to a different use. See that squeeze chute that connects the two corrals? *That* doesn't look so old.'

A tingle washed across her skin. 'No,' she muttered. 'It doesn't.'

The trail into the yard was rutted and creased with tyre tracks, but the place itself looked deserted, and she said as much.

'Could be that it's not occupied all the time, only when they've got a shipment of cattle coming in that need their brands changing,' he speculated.

'Well, that should make it a bit easier

for us to take a look around.'

'Sure. Provided it *is* deserted,' he reminded her. 'I think we'll just keep an eye on things for a while before we make our move.'

At Gil's insistence they kept the ranch under observation for the next hour, but in all that time they neither saw nor heard anything to suggest that the place was occupied. Above them, the sun slid westward, leaving the sky a curious, beautiful mixture of pink and purple. At last, Gil rolled onto one side so that he could face her.

'Okay,' he said. 'Give me your camera and I'll go see what kind of proof I can find for you.'

She frowned at him. 'What?'

'You don't think I'm letting you go down there *with* me, do you?' he asked.

'I *do*,' she replied. 'It's my job.'

'It's not your job to take any more risks than you need to.'

'But the place is deserted.'

'We *think* it's deserted.'

'Well, it's still my job. If there's any

evidence to be gathered — '

He raised one hand to silence her, and to her surprise he smiled at her, a crooked smile that softened the worry lines in his face and revealed his white, even teeth. 'It's not going to do me any good to argue with you, is it?' he asked.

Despite her nerves, she returned the smile. 'I'm afraid not.'

He sighed. 'Come on, then. But stay close.'

And without even thinking about it, he took one of her hands in his, the contact between them both comforting and exciting to her. They broke cover and descended the far slope in a crouching run. The cabin below remained quiet, in darkness, and if the place was occupied, then no one there sounded the alarm.

The ground flattened out beneath them, and they ran on for a few more yards before dropping into the shadows of some more boulders. 'So far, so good,' he whispered.

She studied his profile as he in turn

studied the ranch. She could've told him that he no longer had to hold her hand, but had no desire to do so. In that moment they were joined both physically and emotionally, conspirators working towards the same goal, and it was a good, *right* feeling.

Dusk was upon the ranch now. Everything was quiet and still. Gil whispered, 'I think we should check out that barn first. If they're using running irons to change brands, that's where they'll be keeping them.'

Kate nodded. 'All right. You check out the barn, I'll see if I can break into the cabin. There could be ledgers or some other type of paperwork that might prove useful.'

'I'm not so sure that splitting up is such a good idea, Kate.'

'We'll cover twice the ground in half the time,' she argued.

He could see the sense to that. 'All right,' he agreed reluctantly. 'But let's make it quick. We'll meet up again here in fifteen minutes, okay?'

'Okay. Oh, and here.'

He frowned at what she took from her jacket pocket and offered him. 'Disposable gloves? What are they for?'

'The last thing we need to do is contaminate any evidence we *do* find.'

Taking them, he said, 'I guess I was wrong about you, Kate. You really *are* an investigator, aren't you?'

They shared a tight smile.

'And Gil?' she said.

'Yes'm?'

She looked directly into his face, and he into hers. She thought about the way he'd kissed her back in Bluebird Canyon, just after her terrifying encounter with the bull, and wanted to kiss him again. But instead all she said was, 'Good luck.'

He bobbed his head. 'You too,' he replied, adding, 'And be careful. I hate to say this, but I'm kind of getting used to having you around.'

Before she could react, he broke from cover and ran to the wall of the nearest building, the cabin. He stood there for a moment with his back to the wall, but still no one raised the alarm. As she watched, heart in mouth, he edged cautiously to the corner and peered around. When he was satisfied, he crossed the yard at a run. He reached the barn, opened one of its tall double-doors, vanished inside and closed the door behind him.

With her pulses racing, Kate pulled on her own gloves, then half-ran to the cabin, where she dropped to a crouch beside the corner and fished out her bump key. This would open practically any lock, or so she had been informed. Well, she *hoped* it would, anyway.

She crept along the front of the cabin, ducking once when she came to a window, just in case. Around her, the ranch lay silent in the growing gloom. An eternity passed before she reached the door, briefly examined the lock and then went to work with the bump key.

A few moments later her efforts were rewarded with a soft click.

The door was unlocked.

Trying to control her runaway

breathing, Kate opened the door. If anyone should be inside, waiting for her, she had no idea what she'd say or do.

But there came no challenge. The cabin was empty. She closed the door behind her and made a quick but thorough appraisal of her surroundings by flashlight.

The door opened into a large, sparsely-furnished room. In the poor light she'd made out a sofa, a couple of armchairs, a desk, and immediately checked the drawers. She found nothing that would confirm Gil's suspicions about what the place was being used for, and hoped Gil himself was having better luck.

A door in the facing wall led through to a bedroom. There were two single beds, a cabinet, a shelf of books. Kate checked through the cabinet, but once again came up empty.

She was retracing her steps when one of the boards beneath the colourful throw rug on the floor creaked gently under her weight. She didn't pay it any mind at first, but as she reached the door, she hesitated and glanced back frowningly.

On impulse she went back to the rug, brushed it aside and ran her palms over the boards. One stood ever so slightly proud of the rest. She tried to lift it without success, got up and hurried to the small, untidy kitchen, where she went through the cupboards in search of something to help prise the board up.

What she found in one of the cupboards froze her.

Suddenly everything else was forgotten as she played her flashlight over the bottles sitting in a neat row on one of the shelves. Romfidine . . . detomidine . . . xylazine . . . medetomidine.

She let her breath go in a rush, for they were all animal anaesthetics!

But almost immediately she cautioned herself not to jump to any hasty conclusions. The anaesthetics by themselves meant nothing. After all, this *was* a ranch, so they could hardly be considered out of place.

She closed the cupboard door and checked the drawers until she found an old screwdriver. Taking it back into the bedroom, she quickly set to work, trying to lift the loose board in such a way as to leave no tell-tale signs. With the screwdriver, it was the work of mere moments.

Her heartbeat quickened as she shone the flashlight down into the cavity below. The hole contained two packages, each wrapped in cellophane. She reached in and extracted the first. It appeared to be a thick, heavy book. Carefully she removed it from its wrapper. It was brand book, the book in which all legally-registered cattle brands were shown, together with the name and contact details of the brand owners. She flipped through the first few pages, then found what she was looking for.

One of the brands shown in the book had been modified by someone using a pencil. It had started off as a simple X inside a square. But by adding a second square, this one tilted diagonally across the first, the square had become an eight-pointed star cut into sections by the original X. It had become a completely different brand.

She leafed through the rest of the book. Brand after brand had been sketched over and altered, doubtless to assist any would-be rustler in disguising legally-registered brands and obscuring their true origin.

She put the book back in its wrapper, took out the second package. This was smaller than the first, but its contents were no less damning.

'We've got them,' she murmured.

The second package contained a stack of permits giving the bearer permission to transport livestock either interstate or nationally. The permits were counterfeit, of course, but extremely sophisticated for all that.

There could no longer be any doubt in her mind that Gil had been right, that this isolated halfway house *was* being used to re-brand and distribute rustled cattle. She took out her camera and prepared to photograph the evidence she had found. First the brand book, then the fake transport permits, then the animal anaesthetics, which were used, presumably, on the more recalcitrant cattle, whose resistance might otherwise sound the alarm.

But before she could set to work, the room suddenly filled with a sweep of light, then plunged back into darkness.

A pickup had just pulled into the yard and was braking right in front of the cabin.

* * *

For one instant she froze in both mind and body. The worst thing that could possibly have happened *had* happened. The rustlers had returned to the ranch and were even now climbing from their flame-red Dodge Laramie and clattering up onto the covered porch that fronted the cabin!

Her head swam. She couldn't possibly see how she could evade discovery. But there was always the chance. So she threw the book and permits back into the hole and thrust the floor-board back into place, then hurriedly rearranged the throw rug and started for the kitchen, and the back door she'd spotted earlier.

She had no sooner entered the main room, however, than the cabin door clicked open a fraction and one of the rustlers outside said, 'You dummy, you didn't lock the door after you.'

Again Kate froze. The door was ajar, but no one had come in yet. It was only a matter of time, though. She would never make it to the kitchen before the door was opened all the way and she was spotted.

'What?'

'The door wasn't locked.'

'The hell you say. I remember doing it.'

One of the men swore. Clearly he

had just realised what the unlocked door might mean.

'Look lively, you guys! We've had visitors!'

Wide-eyed Kate could only watch in terror as the door began to swing open.

But in the very next moment there came a raucous clatter of tools and buckets from the direction of the barn, and one of the men yelled, *'Over there! The son-of-a-buck's still here!'*

Kate thought, *Gil!* He would never have been so clumsy as to knock something over by accident. That meant he had done it deliberately to draw the newcomers away from the cabin and give her a chance to escape.

Relief washed through her as she broke into a run, entered the kitchen and let herself out through the back door. But her relief was tempered by concern for Gil's safety. If anything should happen to him now . . .

The men at the front of the cabin were in uproar now. Her blood froze when she heard one of them yell,

'*There he is! Get him!*'

She stumbled through the darkness, completely distracted now by her concern for Gil, and came upon the rocks they'd hidden behind more or less by accident. She threw herself down behind them, her breathing loud in her ears, then chanced a look around them, into the ranch yard.

What she saw brought a low moan to her lips.

They had evidently chased and caught Gil as he tried to leave the barn. One of them was dabbing at his mouth with a kerchief, which told her that Gil had put up a fight before being captured.

But be captured he had, for now he was being herded along by two of the four men, and they were holding him by the arms in rough grips that he was unable to break. Furthermore, she could see by the way his head lolled and his footsteps dragged that they had beaten him close to unconsciousness.

Tears stung her eyes. He had

sacrificed himself to give her the chance to get away.

But how could she leave him here, to the mercy of these men? She loved him too much for that.

The thought stopped her in her tracks. Where had that word *love* come from? And yet she knew she could not deny it. Everything about him appealed to her, reached out and struck some kind of physical and emotional chord in her. He was a good man, a strong man, a loyal, selfless, do-right man, and yes, she *did* love him, she loved him for all that and more.

And she would not leave him now.

But what could she do to help him? The rustlers herded him into the cabin and one of them slammed the door behind them. After a moment, light filled the cabin windows. Through one of them she saw the rustler with the busted lip talking urgently into a cell phone. He looked angry, and made agitated gestures as he spoke.

After a moment he rang off. More

lights went on as the rustlers checked through the cabin. She heard one of them call out that the back door had been unlocked.

She was shivering now, as a cocktail of fear, anger and worry for Gil took hold. She felt useless, unable to think of single thing she could do to help Gil the way he'd tried to help her.

Then she remembered the gun she was carrying.

Dare she risk using it? Could she really *bring* herself to use it? What if the rustlers, sensing her indecision, called her bluff?

She didn't know, and that only increased the feeling of uselessness in her.

Think! she told herself. *Make a decision and act upon it! You can't afford to be squeamish now, not when Gil's life is at stake . . .*

Suddenly the cabin door swung open and a yellow bar of light from inside fell out across the porch and the Dodge pickup. A moment later Gil was shoved outside and the four rustlers came out after him. The rustler with the busted lip said, 'All right, Mark. Go lock him in the shed. Rest of you guys, get yourselves set. We got a busy night ahead of us.'

The one called Mark, who wore a dark beard and shoulder-length hair tied in a ponytail, nodded and gave Gil another rough shove. 'Get a move on, mister! Maybe a couple of hours in the shed'll loosen your tongue.'

Gil turned to glare at the man, and it was the state of his face that made all her doubts vanish. They'd beaten him to find out who he was, what he was doing there and what he knew about their set-up, but if Mark's comment was anything to go by, he hadn't spoken a word.

So they'd beaten him. And now, as she looked at him and felt his pain as clearly as if it had been her own, as she looked at his half-closed left eye, at the swelling of his top lip, at the ugly bruise along his jaw, she felt a rush of desire to come to his aid and protect him, and even before she was aware of it.

'Hold it, all of you! Not one move, or I'll shoot!'

She came out of hiding with the gun held tight in both hands and thrust ahead of her. The men in front of the cabin reacted immediately, spinning in her direction, then stopping dead when they saw the weapon in her grasp, and her apparent willingness to use it. Gil's surprise showed clearly for one brief moment. Then it turned to one of anger, and then open admiration.

'Get your hands up!' she snapped. 'I mean it!'

The man with the busted lip now allowed it to curl in disdain. 'Know something, lady?' he asked. 'I don't believe you *do*.'

He took a step in her directly, his free hand reaching forward for the weapon, and she reacted instinctively.

She did the one thing she never thought she'd do.

She squeezed the trigger.

9

The gun went off with a roar that was much, much louder than she'd been expecting, and it made her flinch and jerk the weapon at the moment of discharge. For a split second her eyes screwed shut and she took an involuntary step back. In the very next instant, however, she was back in control of herself, and Busted Lip was staring at the broken earth between his feet, which her bullet had just ploughed up. He looked pale and shaken.

'Hey, now . . . ' he began.

'Shut up!' she said, her voice sounding shrill now, on the edge of cracking all together. 'Put your hands up, all of you! Which of you has got the keys to the pickup?'

No-one replied.

'Which one?' she barked, and taking aim at Busted Lip's chest, she said, 'Tell me, or I'll shoot!'

He hesitated. He was a big brute of a man with a harsh crew-cut and the face of a boxer who'd never quite managed to dodge all the punches, and she could see by the look in his dark eyes that he knew she was bluffing. But there was an element of doubt there, as well. What if she *wasn't*?

To convince him, she thumbed back the hammer.

'Carl,' he called without taking his eyes off her.

The rustler called Carl, a shorter, lighter man with a narrow face, said, 'Are you — ?'

'Give her the keys!' barked Busted Lip.

Kate drew a breath. Her heart was pounding so hard that she was scared she might pass out. But she couldn't, not now.

She said, 'Gil? Are you okay to drive?'

He tore the keys from Carl's fingers. 'Oh, I can drive, all right,' he muttered.

She swallowed. 'All right, you men.

Get down on your bellies and put your hands behind your heads!'

Mark swore. '*What?*'

'Do it!' growled Gil, part-way across to the pickup. 'Believe me, mister, the last thing you want to do is make the lady mad at you!'

To her immense relief, the rustlers did as they were told, albeit reluctantly, stretching out on their stomachs and folding their hands across the backs of their heads.

'You'll never get away with this,' warned Busted Lip.

Kate made her way around to the passenger-side door of the Dodge, keeping the rustlers covered all the way. 'Watch us,' she said with a confidence she didn't feel. 'Ready, Gil?'

Gil had already eased his punished body into the driver's seat and was familiarizing himself with the controls of the four-wheel drive. 'Ready,' he said, and turning the key in the ignition, brought the powerful engine roaring to life.

Kate slammed the door behind her and Gil floored the accelerator. The Dodge spun in a tight circle, spraying dirt up from beneath its thick tyres, then surged forward, taking the trail back out of the box canyon at speed.

It was full dark now, but the pickup's headlights showed them the trail ahead. It was a narrow, rutted dirt road bordered by brush and trees. Further back rose craggy slopes. The road — such as it was — twisted like a restless serpent, and Gil had to decelerate constantly in order to negotiate all the bends safely.

They drove in silence for awhile. Then Gil threw her a quick, worried glance. 'You okay?' he asked.

She offered him a shaky nod. 'I *will* be.'

'That was quite some stunt you pulled back there. Took guts.'

'I couldn't just leave you,' she said simply.

'I'm glad you didn't,' he confessed. 'And I didn't for one minute believe that you would, although I wanted to give you the chance.' He took another bend with a protesting squeal of brakes. The Laramie rocked wildly, throwing her sideways against him. He winced.

'Are you all right?' she asked.

'Sure. They roughed me up a little, but I'll live. Besides, I found you some of that evidence you were after.'

'What was it?'

'Animal hair-clippers,' he replied. 'Rice-root brushes. And liquid nitrogen.'

'Liquid — ?'

He silenced her with a confirming nod. 'They shave the coat around the original brand and then use the liquid nitrogen to freeze-brand a new mark,' he explained.

'I found some evidence of my own,' she offered, bracing herself against the dashboard to minimize the rocking and swaying of the speeding pickup. 'A brand book, phoney transport permits, drugs to knock out troublesome animals. But our friends back there turned up before I could take photos.'

'Never mind,' was his response. 'Our testimony alone should be enough to convince your bosses.'

'That's true enough.'

'Besides . . . '

'What?'

'Well, from what I overheard of their conversation, the rustlers are expecting another shipment of rustled stock in tonight.'

Kate thought quickly. So that's what Busted Lip had meant when he reminded his companions that they had a busy night ahead of them!

'Do you think they'll call it off, now that they know we're on to them?'

'They might do,' he decided. 'All it will take is one phone call. And we forgot to confiscate their cell phones.'

She shook her head. 'I should have thought to do that. I guess I'm not much of an investigator after all, am I?'

'You'll do to the ride the river with,' he returned, and she knew that, in saying that, he had just paid her the greatest compliment it was possible for a cowboy to pay.

'I'm sorry you got involved in this,' she murmured, and meant it.

'*I'm* not,' he replied. 'It's about time someone did something to break this rustling ring once and for all, and I think we might just have done it.'

She was about to open her mouth and thank him for his help and encouragement when instead her eyes suddenly went wide and she screamed, '*Gil! Look out!*'

They had just swept around another hairpin bend in the trail only to find headlights bearing down on them from the opposite direction. Looking beyond them, Kate had just enough time to see a massive Mack Granite truck hauling an equally enormous two-deck livestock trailer behind it, and tell herself that this was probably the shipment the rustlers had been expecting.

Then the driver of the Mack sounded his horn. It was a loud, urgent blare in the darkness.

Gil yanked hard on the steering wheel and the pickup left the road and began to bounce and careen through bush and rocks, while the Mack and its two-deck trailer rumbled past in a blur of speed.

The next half-minute became a crazy blur of noise and movement. The pickup lurched to the left, then right, then left again. Branches scraped and clawed at the windshield as it splintered and cracks began to tear across it like spider webs. There was another sickening lurch, but this time the pickup kept turning over, onto its roof, onto its opposite side, back onto its wheels with a grinding of metal and a shattering of glass. Then —

The Laramie bounced once more, jostling its passengers cruelly, then fell still, its hood crumpled like tinfoil, steam rising skyward from its cracked engine. The smell of gas filled the air. It puddled around the back of the vehicle, the puddle growing wider, deeper, by the moment.

Somehow Kate fought down the pain of a dozen scattered hurts and said, 'Gil . . . '

She felt his hands questing for her in the darkness. 'I'm here, Kate. You okay?'

'I . . . I think so.'

'Then let's get out of this contraption.'

Kate tried her door. It was buckled, and the release wouldn't work. 'I can't open the door.'

'Here,' he said. He twisted at the waist and had to kick at his own door three or four times before it would open. At last it flew back with a wrench of twisted hinges and he slid out, then reached back to help her.

There was no sign of the livestock truck. It had just kept going, most probably because the driver didn't want to get involved in any subsequent accident inquiry with a trailer full of rustled cattle to try and explain away. After the ear-splitting sound of the crash, the night was now frighteningly silent, and that wasn't all. The smell of gas was even more pungent. One spark and it would ignite and take the pickup — and them — with it.

Grabbing her hand, Gil said, 'Come on,' and began to lead them up the near bank onto the rough ground above. 'We've got to put some distance between us and our pals back there. Now they know we're afoot, there's no way they're going to let us get back to civilisation alive. We know too much.'

She was silent for a long while. She had already reached the same conclusion, but having him actually *voice* it really brought it home to her. 'We better not let them catch us, then,' she said at last.

They were on the far side of the ridge when the pickup finally blew. There came a sudden roar and a flash of light, and a rush of hot air that shoved them down the slope and forced them to seek shelter among some nearby rocks as shards of metal rained down everywhere.

Gil, she realised, made sure he covered her body with his own.

After a few moments all they could hear was the crackle of flames as the remains of the Laramie was consumed by fire. Then Gil stood up and thrust a hand down to her. 'We've got to get moving,' he said again.

'Where to?'

'It'll take us days to walk out of here. We have to get back to the horses.'

'But how will we find our way?'

Surprisingly he grinned at her. 'Lord,' he said, 'I can see you're a city girl.'

She placed her hands on her hips. 'Meaning?'

'Meaning we don't need any street-signs out here. It's a clear night, and the stars'll guide us.'

She shivered, for the night was cold. But keeping on the move would also warm her up. So they set off side by side, picking their way across rocky slopes that were lit only by cool moonlight, the sounds of their boots scraping shale an over-loud, unnerving sound.

They walked for perhaps an hour. Kate had absolutely no idea where they were, but Gil seemed to know where they were going. Her feet ached, her legs ached, and it suddenly dawned on her that she was hungry and thirsty. She was tired almost beyond belief and absolutely terrified at the prospect of being caught by the men who even now must be pursuing them.

To take her mind off things, she glanced up at Gil's profile and said softly, 'Did you mean what you said earlier?'

'I generally mean what I say,' he replied. 'What are you talking about, anyway?'

'Oh, nothing.'

'Come on, out with it.'

She held back a moment, feeling foolish again. Then she said, 'That you were getting used to having me around.'

He frowned. 'Did I say that?'

'Uh-huh.'

'Are you *sure*?'

'Of course I'm sure.'

He shook his head. 'I can't recall it. Maybe I said something that just sounded like that.'

She faced front again. 'Maybe you did,' she replied tartly.

He laughed quietly, the last sound she expected to hear from him just then, and when she turned her head to look up at him again, he said, 'Of course I meant it.' But then he added, 'Not that you'll be around for long.'

She shivered again. 'Does that mean you don't think we're going to get out of this alive?'

'It means that when all this is over, you're going to go back to the Cattle Raiser's Association, and I'm going to be out of a job.'

'Is that what you want?' she prodded carefully. 'For me to go back?'

'What I want or don't want doesn't really come into it,' he pointed out. 'Once this is over, I'll be an even poorer prospect than I am now. I wouldn't want to saddle *any* woman with that.'

'All right,' she said. 'So you'll be out of a job. Are you telling me a top-hand like you can't find another one?'

'I'm telling you that the ranching business gets smaller every year. There's just not the jobs anymore. Besides, who's ever going to want to hire a man who sent his last boss to prison?'

'You could always go into business for yourself, you know.'

'Excuse me?'

'I'm thinking of that spread you bought when you were dating Lynne. People will always need horses, especially horses broken to the saddle the way you do it, with patience and compassion. Or are you telling me that dream disappeared when *Lynne* disappeared?'

He stopped so unexpectedly that she walked on a pace or two before she realised. 'It did,' he said, when she turned to face him. 'Until *now*. Until *you*.'

Around them the night went totally

silent. She stood immobile before him, looking up at his broad-shouldered silhouette, thinking about what he'd just said and what it meant to her. All she could see of him were the tiny pinpricks of moonlight that sparkled in his eyes. And then she stepped forward into his arms.

Their kiss was a desperate, urgent meeting of lips. He folded her tightly to him and her hands came up to spread palms-flat against the muscles that bunched either side of his spine.

They broke apart, kissed again almost immediately, but this time it wasn't just one kiss, it was a whole series of little, exploratory pecks, with each as reluctant to relinquish their hold as the other.

A few moments later Kate husked, 'Hold me, Gil. Hold me forever.'

But he didn't. He held her at arms length and grinned at her instead. 'You make the darnedest requests at the darnedest times, you know,' he said.

And when she thought about it, she

saw that he was right, and laughed. It was a relief to laugh after everything they'd been through this long, cold night, and when she came into his arms again it was simply so they could be together and hold each other close, to squeeze each other affectionately and know that this was neither the time nor the place for anything more.

'I don't want you to rush in to anything,' he said speaking gently into her hair. 'I don't want you to say anything now you might regret later.'

'I won't.'

'But you might. It's been a heck of a night. I wouldn't blame you for having second thoughts once it's all over.'

'I'll *never* have second thoughts about you,' she assured him in a whisper. 'Or how I feel about you.'

'Well,' he said, 'when this is all over and the dust has settled, you come on out to my place for a couple of days and see what you think of it. I reckon we could make a go of it, the two of us.'

A new and troubling thought occurred

to her. 'You're not just saying it, are you Gil? Because you think it might help me hold myself together till we can get help?'

'You don't listen, do you?' he asked. 'What did I say barely five minutes ago?'

'That you generally mean what you say.'

'Does that answer your question, then?'

'I guess.'

'Oh, you *guess*, do you?'

'No. It does. Beyond any doubt.'

He gave her another squeeze. 'Looks like we're stuck with each other then.'

'And happy to be so.'

'*Overjoyed* to be so.'

'Whoa, boy. No need to overdo it.'

Some of his good humour faded as he took another glance at the stars. 'Come on, then. We still got a fair piece of travelling ahead of us.'

It was a long, dark night, and the country was hard on them both. But they kept putting one foot ahead of the other, knowing that they could do nothing else, not if they wanted to evade capture, make it back to civilisation and alert the authorities to what they'd found at the halfway house.

At last the sky began to lighten away to the east. Gil saw it first, stopped and pointed towards it. Dawn. The start of a new day. Somehow it put new life into Kate, into *both* of them.

An hour later they came down into a twisting canyon, and Kate cried, '*Look!*'

There ahead was the natural rock bridge that spanned the canyon, and which had caught her attention the previous day.

He nodded. 'We're not far now, Kate. I doubt we're more than a mile or two from the horses.'

For the first time she allowed herself to believe that they might actually make it yet. They pushed on, sore-footed but more determined than ever, and as they walked they walked hand in hand, the contact between them a natural thing that required no conscious thought.

A couple of hours later the familiar

stand of junipers came into sight, and as they covered the last few yards to the tree line, they heard the horses begin to stamp and whinny in anticipation of their arrival. Finding new reserves of energy, Kate and Gil broke into a trot, wove through the trees until they spotted the tethered horses in the clearing directly ahead.

Kate said with a heavy sigh of relief, 'We made it! Gil, we *made* it!'

But before he could reply, a new voice snapped, 'Not quite, Kate. Now get your hands up, the pair of you!'

10

They saw too late that they had blundered into a trap, that their pursuers had guessed that they had left horses close by, and that after the car crash, all they needed to do was wait until they returned for them.

For a moment the anger and disappointment that came with the realisation threatened to engulf Kate entirely.

The clearing amid the junipers that had so recently appeared quiet and peaceful now came to life as Busted Lip, Mark, Carl and the fourth, nameless rustler broke cover and surrounded them. Neither were the rustlers alone: as Busted Lip used the gun in his fist to urge them forward, Glenn and Blanche Keyes also appeared, both looking grim and decidedly ill-at-ease.

'Check them for weapons, Lon,' said

Keyes, addressing the fourth rustler.

Lon, a stocky man who looked part-Indian, patted them down roughly, took Kate's gun and stuffed it into his waistband.

'Gil,' Keyes said, shaking his head woefully. 'You were my top-hand. I *trusted* you.'

Gil snorted. 'You trusted *me?* Keyes, I trusted *you* at first, and I wanted to go on trusting you, even when I realised you were behind all this rustling! I thought you and your wife were good folks — '

'We *were!*' snapped Blanche, looking close to tears. 'We *are.* But being 'good folks' doesn't always pay the bills. We were in trouble, Gil. We would have lost everything if the bank had had its way. We were desperate — '

'So you started rustling.'

'That wasn't our idea,' said Keyes. 'The idea was put to us by . . . someone else. Someone who made his living by getting people like us to hold his stolen cattle someplace remote, and turn a blind eye while they were re-branded and then sent out elsewhere. It was *money*, Gil, and it got us out of a financial hole! We had to do it, otherwise we'd have lost everything, and you and all the others would have been out of a job!'

Gil's mouth tightened. Perhaps under different circumstances he could've felt sorry for them. But these *weren't* other circumstances, and he had four guns pointed at him and the woman he loved to prove it.

'So what happens now?' he asked.

Keyes sighed again. 'I wish I knew.' It was clear from his expression that he hated the position in which he now found himself. He and Blanche both were hopelessly out of their depth, and Keyes needed to talk, to get everything out in the open, just to hold their nerve.

Sensing as much, and knowing that the longer she kept him talking, the longer she delayed the inevitable conclusion, Kate took a breath and said, 'You knew I was with the Cattle

Raiser's Association right from the start, didn't you?'

Glenn and Blanche exchanged a glance. 'Not right away,' confessed Glenn. 'But there was always the chance someone would come snooping around sooner or later, so we always made it a point to check everyone out as and when they arrived. Blanche looked through your luggage and found that gun. She fetched it to show me, put it back the following day. Did you miss it?'

Kate shrugged. 'Does it matter?'

'I guess not. Anyway, it was the gun that first alerted us. And after that it wasn't difficult to find out who you really were. You'd paid for your vacation by credit card. When I checked out your bank details, I saw that your salary was paid by the C.R.A.'

'So you tried to get rid of me?'

He nodded. 'Lon here fired a shot to spook your horse into throwing you. We wanted you to have an accident — though not a fatal one. The idea was that you'd injure yourself and have to go home, or maybe lose your nerve and leave of your own free will.'

'But you didn't,' Blanche continued. 'So we made another try with the bull in Bluebird Canyon.' Anger suddenly tightened her features again. 'We didn't want it to come to this! We didn't want to hurt *anyone*.'

'But now . . . ?' prodded Gil.

'Now,' said Keyes, 'you don't leave us much choice.'

'Oh, we could try to bribe you,' said Blanche, 'but we know you well enough by now, Gil, to know that you're your own man, and not for sale. We have to assume the same for you Kate. Besides, even if we took a chance on you, there'd always be the possibility that you'd talk later, and that's a risk we couldn't take.'

'So you're going to kill us?' growled Gil.

Keyes, suddenly unable to speak, could only nod his head.

'You'll never get away with it.'

'Maybe not. But we have to try. You two took a shine to each other and ran off. That's the story we'll tell.'

'It's a thin one.'

'But it's the only one we've got. And it'll buy our . . . benefactor . . . the time he needs to close down the operation here. Your people can suspect whatever they like, Kate, but they'll never be able to prove a thing.'

'They might not *have* to,' said Kate.

Blanche's eyes narrowed. 'What does that mean?' she asked, her voice a little high, unsteady.

'Look at you both,' Kate went on. 'You've no stomach for this, and that's to your credit. Have us killed, and it'll play on your minds from now till the day you die. Sooner or later you'll *have* to tell someone, because you won't be able to live with yourselves unless you do.'

'*Shut up!*' barked Keyes.

'I'm only trying to stop you from making things worse,' Kate persisted. 'At the moment you can be prosecuted for rustling. Do *this*, or order it done, and it'll be murder.'

'*Shut up, I said!*' yelled Keyes. 'You two know too much. What other choice do we have?'

'Turn state's evidence,' she said urgently. 'Help us put away this 'benefactor' you keep talking about, and it'll go easier on you . . . '

'Keyes . . . ' Busted Lip growled warningly. 'Don't get any ideas about crossing the boss.'

'I'm not!' grated Keyes. But for one split second Kate felt that she'd gotten through to the man, offered him a way to avoid what he had been so convinced must be done.

In the very next moment, however, that hope died. Looking thoroughly miserable, Keyes said, 'All right, Lon. Get it over and done with.'

Kate looked up at Gil. He looked as grave as she felt. Their eyes met. Then Kate's mouth moved silently. She said, *I love you.*

Gil replied in kind. *I love you too.*

Then he lashed out with his left forearm, knocking Lon's gun hand skyward. Lon, caught entirely by surprise, squeezed the trigger by reflex and the automatic in his fist sent a shot into the branches overhead.

By then Gil was yelling, *'Run for it!'* to Kate, and fighting to tear the gun from Lon's hand.

Eyes wide, Blanche screamed, *'Stop him! Stop him!'*

Busted Lip was already racing to Lon's aid, but Kate couldn't allow that to happen. Instead of making a run for it, she stuck her foot out and Busted Lip stumbled but didn't quite fall.

He spun around just as Kate ran for the edge of the clearing, and snarling a curse went after her. She fell, or *appeared* to, and when he saw that, a cold, satisfied grin crossed his boxer's face. He shoved his gun away, grabbed her shoulder and roughly began to haul her back to her feet.

To his surprise, Kate offered no resistance, and as soon as she was back on her feet, he saw why.

She had spotted a stout branch which had fallen from a nearby tree and lay half-hidden in the undergrowth. As Busted Lip dragged her back to her feet, she grabbed the branch, holding it in both hands like a club.

He said, 'What — ?'

And then she swung it with all her strength, and the rustler collapsed in a heap, unconscious.

Gil, meanwhile, had succeeded in wresting the automatic from Lon's grip and used the butt to knock his opponent to the ground, where he lay clutching his jaw and moaning.

Once again Kate's eyes met his, and this time there was a message of hope in their gaze, that maybe they might get out of this yet.

Then the rustler called Carl yelled, '*Hold it!*' and she realised he had drawn his own gun and had it pointed in her direction. 'Drop it!' he bawled.

The rustler called Mark, meanwhile, had Gil covered, and was already snatching Lon's automatic from his hand.

Defeat tasted foul in her mouth, but she knew she had no choice but comply. Shaking from the recent action, she threw the branch aside and came back to the clearing.

'You're not making this any easier on yourselves,' Keyes said almost petulantly.

'I could say the same about you,' replied Kate, treating Glenn and Blanche to a withering stare.

'Carl,' Keyes said tiredly. 'Just get it done.'

'Yeah,' said a new voice. 'You *do* that, Carl. If I don't plug you first.'

The rustler spun toward the sound of the voice just as a new figure came out of the surrounding brush with a short-barrelled rifle braced against his hip.

'Now, why don't you all throw down your weapons and reach for the sky?'

Kate's head swam, for it was none other than Randall Woodward!

He was the last person she'd been expecting to see, but right at that moment she could think of no-one she would rather have standing there.

'You two okay?' he asked without taking his eyes off the startled Keyes and their surly henchmen, who were treating him to venomous glares.

'Sure,' said Gil. 'But what the heck are *you* doing here?'

Randy grinned. 'Up until yesterday afternoon, little Miss Kate here was part of my group of hikers. When she said she felt poorly, I told her to take the trail back to the ranch. But when I used my cell phone to check and make sure she'd gotten back safely, they told me they hadn't seen hide nor hair of her.'

He shrugged. 'Well, since she was in my care when she went missing, I fetched the group back to the ranch and set out to find her. I was just about to give up when I heard those gunshots just now.' And then, with remarkable

194

understatement, he said, 'Looks like I showed up just in time, don't it?'

Gil nodded wearily. 'I never thought I'd ever be so glad to set eyes on your ugly face, that's for sure.' And then, sincerely, 'Obliged, Randy.'

'Yes,' Kate agreed. 'I think I've probably misjudged you, Randy.'

'You wouldn't be the first.'

'Are you still carrying your phone?' she asked.

'Right here.'

'Then let's call the police and wrap this up once and for all,' she said, taking the phone when he fished it from his pants' pocket.

Glenn Keyes was watching her with scared eyes. 'Wait!' he said. 'Please! Miss Weaver! Kate!'

She turned to him. 'I don't think we've got anything left to discuss, do you?' she asked.

He licked his lips. 'I think we *have*,' he replied.

His wife murmured frowningly, 'Glenn . . . ?'

'About wh-what you said just now . . . about turning state's evidence . . . It'll go in our favour, won't it?'

She nodded. 'I think so.'

His eyelids fluttered. 'All right, then,' he said. 'If we can agree a deal, I'll tell you everything you want to know.'

★　★　★

Whistling softly, John Kelton grabbed his fishing gear and descended to the ground floor of the ranch house, his basket over one shoulder, his rod balanced across the other. The fishing had always been good at Meadow Spring Ranch. That was one of the reasons he'd always liked the place.

He got about halfway down the stairs before he saw Kate and Gil in the hallway below, waiting for him.

He slowed to a halt then, called down pleasantly enough, 'Morning all. If you don't mind me saying, you two look like you've been dragged through a hedge backwards.'

Ignoring the observation, Gil said, 'Going fishing, Mr Kelton?'

Kelton bobbed his head. 'Plan to get an early start.'

'I'm afraid it'll have to wait,' said Kate. 'You see, we've been doing a little fishing of our own, and it appears that we've caught *you*.'

His eyebrows met in the middle. 'What's that? I don't under — '

'I think you do,' Gil cut in flatly. 'You're behind all this rustling, aren't you, Kelton? You go around and enlist the services of ranchers like the Keyes to keep your operation running. Ranchers who are greedy enough or desperate enough to let you use their ranches to hide and re-brand your stolen stock until it can be moved on.'

Kelton's eyes went round. '*What?* That's a darned lie!'

'Not the way Glenn and Blanche Keyes tell it,' said Kate. 'You're through, Mr Kelton. And so is your lousy business.'

Kelton sneered down at them. 'What

is this? A citizen's arrest?'

'No sir. The police are already here and ready to make it official. I just wanted to have the pleasure of telling you personally that it's all over.'

Kelton was shaking now, his eyes shuffling from Kate and Gil to the window beside the door, beyond which he could now see a blue and white car from the county sheriff's office.

'Well,' he rasped in a low voice, 'I trust you enjoyed your moment of glory?'

Kate nodded. 'Actually,' she said, 'I *did*. Now, I think you'd better go back to your room. The police will want to charge you formally in a while.'

★   ★   ★

At last, it was over. Kate had done what she'd set out to do, and more besides. But all that she could think about now was how tired and hungry and how thirsty she was. And how much in love.

She turned to find Gil smiling down

at her, and opened her arms to him. 'Hold me?' she asked.

He lifted one eyebrow. *'Forever?'* he countered.

She nodded. 'Forever.'

Still he held back. 'Forever's a long time, you know,' he teased.

'It'll never be long enough, as long as I'm with you.'

He grinned. 'Then I guess we better get started right away.'

They embraced, and that was exactly the way she wanted it to be. Her and her man, holding each other.

Forever.

THE END